Divided

They

Fall

Regina A. Blackburn

iUniverse, Inc.
New York   Bloomington

Divided They Fall

iUniverse books may be ordered through booksellers or by contacting:

iUniverse
1663 Liberty Drive
Bloomington, IN 47403
www.iuniverse.com
1-800-Authors (1-800-288-4677)

ISBN: 978-1-4502-4915-7 (sc)
ISBN: 978-1-4502-4916-4 (e)

Printed in the United States of America

iUniverse rev. date: 10/6/2010

"What's done in the dark
Will come to light"

Thank you:

1. Dolly, for reading and listening at all times

2. Nino, for the early encouragement

3. Delois, for your enthusiasm and suggestions

4. C.J., for that April telephone call (you know the one), and

5. Tanya, for your vision of my wonderful book design

And to all of my family and friends, who I regard as my extended family, thanks for your faith IN me, your support OF me, and your love FOR me.

Chapter 1:

I was running late to catch my plane to Atlanta. I called my best friend, Jerome, last week to tell him to make himself available for my Friday evening arrival there. I wasn't eligible for vacation for another five months; however, when my boss said that he needed someone to go to Atlanta to get a client's signature for some court documents, I jumped at the chance. Because of their money-conscious mentality, they had already tried handling the matter via fax, but in this case, a fax would not be admissible in court. Great! Justice has been served! I have a few college friends in Atlanta that have suggested to me on more than one occasion to look into employment possibilities there, but I never followed up on it, hoping that my current situation with the law firm would improve. Now, I'm not so closed-minded to the idea. As a matter of fact, my plan now is to work a few more months with the firm then get the hell out! Hainesworth, Fascell & Younger don't appreciate my talents and I'm tired of trying to convince them what a gem they have in me. Getting the client's signature in Atlanta should not take more than an hour, at the most, then the rest of the weekend trip belonged to me. Perfect planning!

From Atlanta's International Airport, I called Jerome to let him know that the flight was in, and as usual, he was there. He and I had attended Howard University in Washington, D.C. together. It seems like we've always been close. Jerome is now a stock broker for Rubenstein & Craft, a major brokerage firm in Atlanta. He has done extremely well for himself, and as a result, for Rubenstein & Craft. He's advanced to become one of their most valuable employees. Unlike me, he is doing something that truly makes him happy, and getting the BIG BUCKS for it. During college, Jerome had a terrible reputation for being a lady's man; so much so that I penned him the nickname of 'rome'. It was actually 'roam', because of his many infidelities. He had so many women available to him that he maintained a chart that hung on the inside door of his closet that kept track of who's who and who did what. I used to think it terrible of him, being such a womanizer, but I later come to realize that Jerome could only do what they allowed him to do, and judging from the information on his closet door, he didn't have many saying no... to anything! Everyone always assumed that he and I were more than friends because we were always around one another, but they were wrong. Jerome and I understood each other perfectly and could discuss anything: relationships, business ideas, desires, fears, dreams, personal baggage... anything! He stood about 6'6", light brown complexion, close cropped hair, and beautifully bowed legs that you could dream of slipping in between. He had the cutest dimples on his cheeks and was in excellent physical condition. Jerome was a great swimmer and competed on the University's swim team, where he won scores of medals and trophies. As a result of this activity, he had an incredibly massive chest, and arms that were equally impressive. What woman could ask for more? His only vice was that untamed libido that seemed insatiable. He was not very committed to any one woman, unfortunately, but was still a good man. No doubt some lucky woman would snag him one day and become a very happy B.I.T.C.H. (Black In The Comfort Hemisphere).

"Raven! Hey baby! You look great! Must be someone real special in D.C. that's keeping you looking so luscious and happy." Jerome said.

He reached out and embraced me. Damn, that felt good! He took my overnight bag and we proceeded to walk to his car.

"And how have you been Rome? You been keeping the ladies happy down here in the southland?" I asked, but already knowing what his response would be.

"Baby, if the honey's were any sweeter, I'd have diabetes."

We both laughed. I gave him the address of my firm's client and we were on our way to his office. I was to meet the client by 4:30pm, and fortunately enough for me, I was right on schedule. After getting the signature, I re-entered Jerome's car.

"Hey babe, I got a surprise for you."

"Really? What is it Rome?" I said inquisitively.

"I'm now living in the Sarafian Skydome!"

"You're kidding! The Sarafian?"

"Yeah." he said proudly, smiling so wide that it accentuated his beautiful dimples.

"When did all of this happen?"

"A few days ago." he said beaming.

"Why didn't you call me?" I asked.

"Well, I thought I'd surprise you. I hope you like it."

"I like it already."

The Sarafian is a very posh condo community. I remember being invited to a party there a few years ago. I left there three days later after what turned out to be a very wild private party between me and some guy. I don't remember his name, but I can never forget his condo: four bedrooms, two fireplaces (one in the living room and one in the master bedroom), a Jacuzzi, one and one half baths, and a spectacular picture window that extended across the entire wall of his living room! It was quite a view. I remember it well.

Rome's condo was immaculately decorated in lacquered furniture and coordinated rugs. The walls were sprinkled with expensive artwork that made me nervous. I felt like I was in a museum or something, afraid to touch anything for fear that I'd damage it. It was beautiful!

"Raven, you can stay in any bedroom you'd like, except of course the master. That's FOR the master."

"How generous of you, master asshole." I said jokingly. "Thanks. Hey, did you call the gang to tell them I'd be in town today?"

"I'm one step ahead of you babe. They'll be here around ten-ish."

"Now you're talking!" I said with excitement. "I miss them all so much."

With the exception of Mitch's wife, Anita, we were all alumni of Howard University and have maintained some degree of communication ever since.

I walked down a hallway and turned a corner. I gasped. The picture window was directly in front of me and I was spellbound. The view of Atlanta's skyline was breathtaking. I walked down a couple of stairs into the sunken living room, just to get closer to the clouds.

3

"See something you like, little lady?"

I jumped, not having heard his footsteps approaching. I'd become hypnotized by the city's magnificence, and stood there with my mouth agape.

"I don't recall the city looking as beautiful", I said in almost a whisper. "Your new place sure does show it off well".

"Yeah, it does, doesn't it."

We both just stared out of the window in silence for what felt like a full minute.

"Hey", Rome said breaking the moment, "there's a new club that just opened up a few months ago that I've grown kinda fond of. It's called Penny Lane. The live jazz is the best around. I know how much you like that." he said smiling.

"That sounds great. I haven't heard good music in a long time. Speaking of good music, have you heard anything from…"

"Well, now that YOU'VE brought it up, I did talk to him about a year ago." Jerome said.

"And?"

"And… well, the man still loves you Raven."

"And how do you profess to know what's in Parker's heart? Doth thou have x-ray vision?" I said facetiously.

"As a matter of fact, I do. Just ask my women." he said smiling.

"C'mon Rome." I pleaded.

"O.K., o.k.! He told me this himself."

I turned my head away from him, trying to prevent him from seeing my face. I felt myself becoming too emotional to not be involved with him anymore.

"You know, he really hurt me."

"I remember," Jerome said, "but what's past is past."

"A typical male line," I said, half serious and half joking, "but I think a part of me will always love him too, but never again like that; never again with any man to that extent!" I said with conviction.

"I can understand that babe. Didn't mean to hit that nerve", as he grabbed me and gave me a head nuggie.

We laughed and it took away some of the seriousness of the moment. I decided to get some rest before the evening's festivities. I told Jerome to wake me around 9p.m. I figured that would give me enough time to dress and I should be nice and refreshed. I laid across the king-sized guest bed and turned on the clock radio that was sitting on the night stand. Whitney Houston was singing 'Didn't We Almost Have It All'. A tear welled in the corner of my eye as a reminder of the pain of me and Parker's time together. I closed my eyes and drifted off to sleep… thinking only of Parker Whitfield and what could have been.

Chapter 2:

I met Parker shortly after graduation from Howard University. Neither Jerome nor I had jobs at the time, so we both agreed that we would "relax" for a few months before life became too complicated. I stayed with Jerome at his parents' home in Atlanta. They loved me and referred to me as the daughter they never had. As for me, they were the parents I hardly remember. We had a wonderful time for those months: hanging out and partying our asses off... nightly. It was a wild and carefree time for us both. Young and irresponsible. Jerome and I stayed in constant trouble; me with the men I'd meet and Jerome with his women. We lived only for the day and nothing was taken seriously.

Jerome was still an avid swimmer and at least twice a week would go to the YMCA to workout. I'd tag along occasionally if I could get up from the night before. This particular morning, I did accompany him. Jerome was really focused on his workout this day, completing lap after lap. I, on the other hand, was on the other side of the pool in the shallow end trying to impress the pre-teens with my panic-stricken crawl and embarrassing breast stroke. I had broken the plane of the water with my breast stroke and had inhaled, preparing to go under again, when I noticed through the fog of my goggles, this figure that appeared to me to be ALL man... and I can't stress that enough! As I went under the water again, I began to freestyle to get to the side rail quickly. I held onto the rail and turned to get another look at him. I moved my goggles above my eyes so that I could see him 'unfiltered', but by then he was nowhere in sight. Did I imagine him? Was there not this gorgeous man standing on the deck with his well-fitting Speedo trunks on? I replaced my goggles over my eyes and resumed my swim routine. Pushing off from the wall, I twisted my body around to do the back stroke. I guess I'd gotten about halfway to the other side when this 'torpedo' wearing red Speedo trunks zoomed past me. Wow! By the time I got to the other side, he'd already done that flip-turn thing that the professional swimmers do so well. I could never get that technique down without banging the heel of my feet on the tile.

"Well, I'm not going to chase him." I thought. "I'll just wait for him to return to this end."

To my surprise, he reached the opposite side of the pool and swiftly lifted himself out.

"What! Where does he think he's going?" I almost said out loud.

I looked away, so as not to stare, but I had my radar targeted on this guy. He was walking toward some bleachers that were on the side of the pool nearest to where Jerome was swimming. I began slowly making my way through the water, coming closer to where they were.

"Are you kidding? Jerome knows this Adonis?", I thought.

Jerome waved, acknowledging him standing on the deck and swam towards him. When Jerome reached the side of the pool, he remained in the water with his arms crossed, resting on the deck floor.

"Cozy? Hey man!" Jerome said excitedly. "When did you get back in town?"

"Back in town... back in town... from where?" I wondered. Then a terrible thought came to me and I cringed with ill ease.

"What if he's been in jail! Please don't let it be jail!"

"I've been back for about a year now", the stranger said.

"That's great man." Jerome said.

"It was a lot of hard work, man, but I think I've learned my lessons well." he replied smiling at Jerome.

"I know that's right man, but hell, you were more than halfway there when you took off." Jerome said.

"So, he was away learning lessons?" I thought. "Then quite naturally he must've been in college, right?" I said trying to convince myself that his absence was a positive one. He appeared to be older than Jerome and I, so maybe he was away in the military? Maybe graduate school. "Yeah", I thought, "that'll work for me... graduate school."

Jerome pulled himself up out of the water and they walked over to the bleachers and out, but now further away from me.

"Damn! Now I can't hear any part of the conversation. Well, I'll just have to crash this reunion." I thought.

I got out of the water and walked toward the both of them, making my presence known before the stranger left.

"Rome, did you bring any suntan lotion with you?", I said knowing full well that he didn't.

"I sure didn't babe," he replied smiling, recognizing my modus operandi.

"I think I've got some in my swim bag in the locker room." the stranger said.

"Do you mind, I mean, I wouldn't want to put you to any trouble."

"Oh, no trouble at all, it would be my pleasure. I'll be right back." the stranger said smiling.

This man had one of those Denzel Washington walks: proud, manly, majestic, confident, and very, very sexy!

"Who the FUCK is he Rome?" I asked, wide-eyed with wonder. "Is he a good friend of yours? Is he a relative? Is he married? Does he have any children? Does he live in town... alone? What?"

Jerome doubled over with laughter. He knew that his friend had piqued my curiosity. It was a must that I see him again outside of this environment.

"Forget it doll", Jerome said, still laughing a little bit. "He's not for you."

"What? Have you taken leave of your senses? What's wrong with him Rome? Is he gay or something like that? Is that it?" I asked tentatively.

"No, he's very much straight, that's part of the problem."

"I don't see that as a problem Rome".

"Look Raven, he's a musician and he travels around a lot. He has so many women, I'M a virgin compared to him. I just don't want to see you hurt babe, that's all. I know this man, and Cozy has done major damage in the past with women. Believe me, I've seen the aftermath of his work many times."

"Well hell, is there anything positive about the motherfucker you can say, Dad?" I asked sarcastically.

Jerome smiled. "He's one helluva musician and a pretty good three-pointer man on the courts. I remember one game, we had only ten seconds left, and Cozy..."

"Rome, I don't give a shit about your basketball game and a 'three-pointer'"! I snapped. "I want to know about the man himself."

"Well all that I can say is that he's brutal with the ladies Raven, and I would prefer you just put the notion out of your mind about you and him." Jerome said.

"Well, I think I'll take a gamble with this one." I said undaunted. "He's fine as hell!"

"I really wish you wouldn't babe. I can't recommend this match, or should I say mismatch."

"Stop being so possessive Rome... it's not very becoming. Besides, I'm a big girl. All I ask is that you give me a proper introduction when he comes back over here and I'll take it from there, o.k?"

"Raven", Jerome said with a sigh.

"Please Rome, do this one for me." I begged.

He was heading back towards Jerome and I, when a woman in a thong bikini approached him and gave him an engulfing hug. I swear, I felt as though I had bionic vision because I zeroed right in on his face. In reading his lips, I think he said something about a stroke. I hope it was a swimming stroke, but somehow I doubt it. She thanked him several times, then hugged him again!

"The nerve of this slut hugging MY MAN!" I thought.

I turned and looked at Rome who was still seated on the bleachers, only to get the 'I told you so' look. I felt awkward and jealous and knew that it was silly for me to feel this way. I had no basis for such an emotion. I don't even know this guy! I walked over to the edge of the pool and dove into the water. I started doing laps as well as Rome did earlier (or at least in my mind I did). I had so much energy all of a sudden that I did almost three laps. As I was making my way back across the pool, he approached Jerome and they resumed talking. When I reached the wall, he yelled out to me.

"Sorry for the delay. I got the lotion for you."

"Fuck you bitch, and your lotion," I thought to myself, smiling all the while. I pulled myself out of the water.

"Thanks, I really wanted to work on my tan today."

"You have such a radiant complexion now," he said, looking at me. "Have you been tanning in the Caribbean?"

"No, I haven't, and thank you." I said graciously, but thinking "why don't you use your lines on 'Queen of the Thongs' at the other end of the pool!

"Jerome, would you do me the honor of introducing me to your beautiful friend?" he said smiling, and looking directly into my eyes without blinking.

"You really think I'm beautiful?" I thought.

Jerome reluctantly proceeded with the intros.

"Parker Whitfield, this is my best girl Miss Raven McNair. Raven, this is my old buddy from the way, Parker Whitfield, or Cozy, as he's known around town."

We were shaking hands while the introductions were taking place and exchanged niceties. Parker was jet black, about Jerome's height, with a very stimulating body, even down to his washboard stomach. His teeth were pearly white, and his smile was warm and inviting. His coal black eyes were riveting, and he had the juiciest-looking lips I'd ever seen in my life. I just know that I'm gonna enjoy tasting them… over and over again… and I WILL get to taste them! I'd never felt this way before. I felt I was losing control of myself.

"Would you like for me to apply the lotion to your back, Raven?" Parker asked.

My eyes diverted to Jerome for a brief moment, then back to Parker.

"Uh, sure, I guess, oh, I suppose that'll be o.k." I said, feeling like an adolescent school girl.

"Wouldn't want you to strain trying to get to those hard-to-reach areas, or worse, not being able to reach them at all and having to do without." he said smiling very seductively.

I felt I had to respond with something a bit more witty than the last fiasco response I gave.

Not skipping a beat I said, "I've never been 'without', Mr. Whitfield, and that statement applies across the board."

We both smiled at one another.

The introduction of Parker Whitfield into my life changed it forever. Parker's influence propelled me into a world that I was not sure that I was ready for. A world of deceit and mistrust, pain and sadness. He forced reality on me. He forced me to become an adult.

Chapter 3:

Regardless of how many times I heard it on the evening newscast or read it in the obituary column of the New Hampshire Vine, it still didn't seem quite real to me. This could not be happening to us, to our family: 'Mr. and Mrs. Vincent T. McNair of Concord, New Hampshire, met with an untimely death when their car careened into an embankment', the obit read. They are survived by their three children; Darlene 12, Raven 6, and Elliott 3. I remember the house being very crowded for what seemed like weeks, with friends and relatives that I'd not seen in years, some I'd not met at all. There was lots of crying and sadness, and everyone was being comforted by one another. All I knew was that I wanted these people out of my house and to have my mom and dad back home. I wanted to hear the sound of my dad yelling 'Honey, I'm home' as he walked through the door from his engineering job, or to feel the warmth of my mother's hand as she stroked my head while reading me a bedtime story. Life as we knew it had changed, but we were too young then to understand the extent of our loss.

My Dad always prided himself as being a thorough man and a good provider for his family. Unbeknownst to my sister, brother, and I, my parents willed us a shit-load of money, nearly a million dollars. Their live insurance policy was divided equally among the three of us and placed in a trust fund that couldn't be accessed until we were twenty-one years old. The remaining funds would go toward paying off the house, burial expenses, and maintenance money for my Aunt Sam and Uncle Adam to take care of us. We weren't spoiled kids by no stretch of the imagination, but I really can't remember a want that wasn't satisfied… except for the return of our loving parents to us. Mom was an elementary school teacher before she and Dad met. After marriage, Mom gave up her teaching career to concentrate on her new role as wife and shortly thereafter, mother.

My mother's sister, Samantha, and her husband Adam became our legal guardians. Aunt

Sam had a striking resemblance to our mom: a tall, buxomed woman with short black hair, beautiful brown eyes, and long slender legs. Her skin was smooth and even-toned. She was gorgeous. Aunt Sam was younger than mom by about eleven years. As a sales representative for a medical equipment company, she traveled the world and always brought us gifts from wherever she went. As you can guess, she was very popular among the McNair children. We didn't get to see Aunt Sam as often as we liked because she lived so far away… some other 'galaxy' called Iowa. The last time we saw Aunt Sam was shortly after her marriage to Uncle Adam. He was an attorney in private practice and doing quite well. His first wife died of complications with diabetes, leaving him to rear two young boys as a single parent. Uncle Adam's sons, Calvin and Peter, were twins. They stayed with us during the week Aunt Sam and Uncle Adam were away on their honeymoon. They weren't that much older than we were, I think they about thirteen or fourteen years old, and we all got along splendidly. It was actually sort of nice to have them around because deep inside, I'd always wanted older brothers.

Living in Iowa was truly a culture shock. This period was traumatic enough for us; dealing with the loss of our parents, being torn away from our friends, our school and teachers, our church, and now forced to become Iowans! It was almost unbearable. Their house, or should I now say 'our' house, was a cape cod that sat on six acres of beautiful meadow. It was wonderful having all of that space to romp and play, but very lonely too. I felt that I didn't have any one there for me. Calvin and Peter were out most of the time with their teenage friends, Elliott was too young, and Darlene had her own set of problems. She was having a much more difficult time with the adjustment than Elliott or me, and took the loss of our parents very hard. I suppose she understood the finality of their death more clearly than me or Elliott could understand. Before their deaths, she was the pride of our household; an 'A' student, an usher in the church, and well liked amongst her peers. Now, she lashes out at everyone, especially towards the kids in our area. She was involved in some kind of ass-kicking nearly everyday! Aunt Sam and Uncle Adam didn't know quite how to handle her; one minute they're punishing her, then the next they're giving her extra attention to appease her. Eventually, it was Uncle

Adam who saw the seriousness of her problem and insisted that she see a psychiatrist. She had bi-weekly sessions after school for three months, at which time the therapist's solution was for Darlene to get involved with some sort of club or activity to give her a sense of belonging. So, following the doctor's advise, Aunt Sam enrolled us both in the fucking Girl Scouts, and Elliott in Little League baseball. I thought the Scouts was great fun and I got along with everyone really well, but Darlene was still having problems in channeling her anger. She constantly fought the other girls, and being her sister, I found myself dragged into a few skirmishes; guilt by association. I think that they thought that I must enjoy fighting too since my sister was so good at it. Although I would do what I could if I 'had' to, Darlene seemed to always have the situation well under control, and would rarely need any help from me. She refused to consider Iowa as 'her home'. In our quiet moments in our bunk beds when we were supposed to be asleep, she would always talk of living someplace else… anyplace else, but not here. After about a year and a half of this behavior, Darlene finally began to settle down.

One day, Aunt Sam discovered a shoe box covered with cloth on the floor of Darlene's closet. Inside she found a collection of writings, mostly militant or sad in tone, that Darlene had written. Aunt Sam, upon reading a few of them, was pleasantly surprised to learn that Darlene had an aptitude for writing poetry. In an excerpt from one of them, Darlene wrote:

> I walk away in horrid rage,
> Into my room, into my cage,
> And there I cry and try to hide,
> The fact that I am sick inside.
> I lay down on my bed awhile,
> And try to formulate a smile,
> But a smile will not come on my face,
> 'Cause I feel alone and out of place.

Darlene had found a niche with which she could channel her energy. She joined the literature club and turned out to be a very talented writer. My Aunt and Uncle were very relieved and happy with Darlene's progress, but she'd also had a year and a half of making enemies from all the ass-whippings she handed out, and some of her victims weren't so forgiving.

One Friday after school, I was waiting for Darlene on the playground. I knew that every Friday she would be late leaving school because she met with her writing club. It was such a beautiful day that day. So much so that when she came out, we decided that we would walk home instead of catching the school bus as we normally did. As we walked, Darlene talked about how excited she was with her club and her new found friends. This was her new beginning, and I couldn't have been happier for her too. I missed my big sister, the one that I knew from Concord. In the distance, we saw a small group of boys, about four or five of them skipping rocks across a lake. When we got near enough, one boy turned and pointed his finger toward us, as we continued walking along the side of the road past them.

"Hey Mike, there's that little bitch that beat up my sister."

The boy turned around to look at us. We kept walking.

"Oh yeah! She beat up my cousin too", another boy added.

"Hey you black nigger! I see that you don't look so tough now," Mike said.

They began to throw rocks at us, barely missing our heads. Darlene and I continued walking, but at a faster pace.

"Y'all better watch those damn rocks!" Darlene said in a very forceful tone. "We're not bothering you."

"And if we don't, what are you gonna do about it?"

"We will tell your mother, that's what!" I said, thinking that this threat would surely strike fear into their hearts, and they'd cease taunting us.

"Fuck you!" another responded.

"Fuck your mama!" Darlene retorted.

'Touché sis", I thought.

"Oh yeah? Let's get them bitches and teach them some manners!"

The boys began running toward us. I thought I was scarred before, but now I was terrified. These boys were much bigger than we were. I'd guess that they were around fourteen or so. It felt as though we were running for our lives. I couldn't help but think that this anger that they felt went far beyond the issue of their family members and Darlene. This was a deep seeded hatred that was developing long before we came to Iowa. Darlene grabbed my hand so as not to leave me behind, but I was so afraid that I kept up with her with no trouble. We were panting by now, as we'd run almost a quarter of a mile. They were gaining on us when we heard the sound of an approaching vehicle. We both turned and looked over our shoulders and saw, to our delight, the school bus. Oh how I love those big, yellow, ugly motherfuckers! To this day, I'm partial to the color yellow. We ran in the middle of the road and flagged the driver down. Within an instant... a split second, a large rock found it's way into Darlene's eye.

"Auuuuuuugggggghhhhh! My eye... oh God, my eye!" Darlene cried out.

She dropped to her knees and covered her eye with her hand. Blood was gushing out everywhere, seeping through her clasped fingers like water through a faucet. She was screaming hysterically.

"You stupid assholes!" I said. "Look what you've done to my sister! You bastards will pay for this shit!" I said, using a vocabulary that I was unaware that I had.

The boys scattered and the bus screeched to a stop. Darlene was covered with blood and sobbing out of control. When the bus driver neared us, a panic-stricken look blanketed his face, as Darlene's eye appeared to be hanging out of it's socket by a string. Despite his shocked exterior, he moved with precision. He jumped out of the bus, scooped Darlene up, yelled for me to get on the bus, and we raced to the nearest hospital. Time was definitely of the essence. I tried comforting my sister, but I was almost in as much pain as she. Darlene was losing a lot of blood and we couldn't stop it. She tried putting her head back, but nothing helped.

"Hang on sweetheart. We'll be there any minute now!" The driver yelled.

He picked up his two-way radio and messaged the school, who in turn alerted the hospital of our arrival. By the time we got there, everything was in place. Emergency surgery had to be performed in order to try and save her eye. Aunt Sam and Uncle Adam arrived soon thereafter.

"Why did this happen?" I thought. "Just when she was trying to do the right thing. Just when she had found herself again."

Aunt Sam stayed with Darlene and instructed Uncle Adam to take me home. I was a wreck. I didn't want to leave her. I had already lost Mom and Dad, I thought.

"Please God, don't take Darlene away from me and Elliott too", I prayed aloud. "Please".

Chapter 4:

Darlene was indeed a different girl by the time she was released from the hospital. Evidently she had a lot of time to think about things and I think it finally sunk in that Aunt Sam and Uncle Adam WERE Mom and Dad for us now for all intent and purposes, that Iowa WAS our home, and that we, Aunt Sam, Uncle Adam, Calvin, Peter, Elliott, and myself were HER FAMILY, and loved her very much. She wore a white patch over he eye for a long time, and had to go back and forth to the hospital for different tests and follow up examinations. She had to wear glasses after that, but what the heck. She had her sight and both her eyes!

There was such an outpouring of concern and well wishes for Darlene from our entire neighborhood when she came home from the hospital. She even had a welcome home party sponsored by the Girl Scouts Association of our area. It was almost like having a celebrity in the house. The girls that had once been her foes were now her friends, and all the ass-kicking and bad feelings seemed to be pushed aside. All seemed forgiven. Those once lonely six acres of meadow surrounding our house were no more. Darlene's friends (and mine too) were over the house constantly. We had slumber parties and barbecues, and as we got older, "social get-togethers". Life was good. Darlene's life was now totally back on track and her grades returned to the straight "A" status of old. It was great having my sister back. Thank you God.

The years that followed went by sort of uneventful compared to that summer. We all graduated from high school, with Darlene graduating Salutatorian of her class. I left home to attend Howard University in

Washington, D.C., majoring in business; Elliott entered the military, and Darlene, ironically, stayed in Iowa and became the Editor-in-Chief of the local newspaper, "The Iowan Express". Isn't it funny how life turns out?

Chapter 5:

Before Parker and I left the YMCA that morning, we made arrangements to get together that evening for dinner. I remember having to scramble to the salon to get a manicure, pedicure, and a facial. I wanted to be flawless that night. The beautician styled a French roll for me that was nothing less than spectacular. I wore a black fitted satin sheath dress with diamond-studded earrings and matching black shoes. As a finishing touch, the scent of Chanel #5 lightly scented my skin. I knew I had it 'going on'! He picked me up promptly at 7:30pm in an old-model Jaguar. Parker took me to a very chic restaurant that played classical music softly in the background. He complimented me on my appearance several times, almost to the point of embarrassment, but that kind of embarrassment I can live with. Our conversation was stimulating and covered the gamut; from music to religion, to education and politics. I learned a great deal about him during dinner: the elder child of two, a Methodist, a member of the Democratic Party, twenty eight years old, and very intelligent and sensitive, which varied greatly from the description and warnings I'd gotten from Jerome earlier. Parker also attended Morgan State University in Baltimore, Maryland, but dropped out during his senior year to join the CJ London Band, a renowned jazz combo. For nearly three years, Parker fine-tuned his craft and recorded several cd's with them. Despite this accomplishment, however, he wanted to try his hand at developing his own band and returned to Atlanta to cultivate his dream. That dream resulted in a five-piece band known as Saega. Saega featured Rachel on keyboards, Will on percussion, Butch on the base guitar, Ozzie on the lead guitar,

Shanai performing vocals, and of course Parker on the sax. Saega was a huge success in Atlanta and had begun to attract a following in the surrounding Southern states. Parker desperately wanted Saega to infiltrate the West Coast market, but unfortunately L.A. hasn't responded the way he'd hoped.

"Enough about me and the band", Parker said. "I could go on for days talking about Saega. Why don't you tell me about yourself, Raven?" he asked smiling. "What is it you want? What is it you're searching for?"

"I don't know that I'm searching for anything in particular Parker, but I guess I want what most people want… to be happy."

"What about companionship, love, fulfillment?" he asked, as the candle flame's reflection flickered in his eyes. "Do these things matter to you?"

"Of course they do. There are things that I want, but I don't think they happen just because you want it to." I said. "I think that all of our destinies have already been written, and we're merely following our script."

"Well, I believe that sometimes you have to divert from this… 'script' and change a few things, you know? I mean, sometimes a person has to rewrite the script in order to MAKE things happen." he said.

"But even still, I continued, "I think that your rewriting of the script is already written too."

Parker smiled and put his index finger up to his temple, as if I had his undivided attention. His beautiful black-eyed stare moved me, and for a brief moment, my mind drifted to the wish of a more intimate setting. I tried, however, to maintain my train of thought.

"You seem to have done quite a bit of thinking on the subject of fate." he said.

"I have. I find it fascinating how things work out; karma, spiritual strength, destiny."

"And what of you and I? Do we have an appointment with destiny?"

My body trembled. I WAS feeling something very special with him, but I didn't want to reveal so much of myself to Parker so soon, just in case he was in fact the cad that Jerome warned me of.

"I'm starving", I said, not responding to his question. "Shall we order?" I said smiling.

He outstretched his large hand which completely engulfed mine as it rested on the table.

"You're pretty sharp… and evasive." he said smiling as he looked around to summon the waiter.

I laughed. He looked so tempting, so handsome. He had on a gray double-breasted suit with pleated gray pants and black wing-tipped shoes. A red silk handkerchief adorned his jacket pocket and his tie was speckled with faint gray and red designs. During dinner we didn't talk very much, but when dinner was completed, we sipped wine and resumed our discussion, but on a more adult level.

"I like you Raven."

"I like you too Parker."

"You know, "Parker said, "had I gone to where I was suppose to have gone today, it would've placed me on the other side of town and I would've missed my opportunity to meet you."

"Well, I'm glad that you had a detour." I said, encouraging his flirtation.

"Is this the 'fate' that you spoke of earlier?" he asked seriously.

"I don't know Parker," I said looking deeply into his eyes, "what do you think?"

"I think that I was fortunate to have gone to the Y today… and I think that you're beautiful."

"That's very sweet of you to say."

"Well, I'm not just saying it, I mean it. You have brains, as well as beauty, and if this is all so apparent to me in just having dinner with you, I shudder to think of what's to come." he said. "I'd like to get to know more about you, if that's alright with you." Parker said looking very seriously.

"I think that can be arranged." I said smiling. "I feel as though I've known you long before today."

"Is that a good thing, or have I become obsolete already?"

"No Parker. It's a plus. I feel comfortable, natural with you."

Parker smiled at me and I don't know if it was due to the wine, the lack of male companionship, or just his smooth approach, but I swear

I saw no one else in the restaurant but him. It was as though I was looking at him through a cylinder.

"Whoa girl", I thought, "things are moving too fast."

I wanted to put on brakes, but damn! The man was definitely 'doing it' for me! We left the restaurant and went to a club called The White Dove Lounge. Parker was well known and well liked there, and a steady stream of people approached our table to talk to him and to say hello.

"How's this Raven? Do you like the Lounge?" he asked.

I couldn't very well tell him that what would actually be more to my liking would be for us to be in a warm Jacuzzi surrounded by candles, so I gave him a respectable, lady-like response.

"Yes, the Lounge was a good choice Parker." I said, but it really wasn't.

It was nearly impossible to have any kind of continual conversation with him, because of the steady flow of people wanting his autograph, or to shake his hand, or to tell him which song was their personal favorite.

"Do you always attract this kind of electricity from people when you go out for the evening?" I asked, trying not to sound selfish of wanting the time with him all to myself, although, in fact, I did.

"Well, usually when I go to the jazz spots, I'm as close to a celebrity as many of them will ever meet. I'm on cd's, I appear on stage, and I tour the country performing. So, they don't mean any harm, they just want to connect." he said, coming to his fan's rescue. "But if it bothers you, we can go somewhere else." he said genuinely concerned with my feelings.

"No, I don't think that'll be necessary." I said, now regretting that I ever brought it up.

We listened to the music in silence, both of us enjoying our separate but, I'm sure, similar thoughts.

"Miss McNair, may I have this dance?" Parker asked.

I smiled, extended my hand, and let him lead me to the dance floor. As we danced, I closed my eyes and let the music and Parker's firm embrace carry me away. I'd always gauged a man's ability to dance with his ability to make love, and I can instantly tell that Parker knows... how to DANCE. His motions were fluid yet sturdy, and very, very sensual. After a while, I finally opened my eyes, only to find that we were the only ones remaining on the floor and everyone was looking at us. My first thought was that my dress was stuck in my pantyhose in the back or something, then it occurred to me that what they were seeing was something special in bloom, and our rhythmic motion on the dance floor was an extension of that.

"What are you doing to me, girl?" Parker said. "I haven't felt this way in years."

"Then I would say, Mr. Whitfield, that you are due." I said in a very provocative whisper. "Wouldn't you agree?"

The music stopped and we returned to our table. Parker walked behind me with his hands around my waist. They felt strong and warm, just like I like 'it'. What felt like hours of dancing had only been about fifteen minutes or so. Parker motioned to the waiter to bring over another bottle of wine.

"You dance well. You surprised me." he said as he popped the cork of the bottle and poured me a glass.

"How can I surprise you when you don't know me yet." I said.

Parker smiled.

"We've only known one another for about eight hours Parker. You can't possibly know what I can do in just eight hours."

"Oh no?" he asked.

"No." I replied. "There's much more to me than can be absorbed in such a short amount of time." I said seductively.

"Mmm, I like the way you put that," he said as he poured me another glass of wine. "Have you always been so… expressive?"

"Every chance I get" I said with a naughty grin.

We both laughed. We sipped wine, enjoyed the music, and discussed ideas for late night possibilities. To be honest, neither of us wanted the evening to end this soon. We danced a few more times, then departed the club. After that, things seemed much like a fantasy. We boarded a horse-drawn carriage for a midnight ride of the city. It was magical! Parker's broad shoulders supported my head as we nestled back on the cushion of the carriage. He leaned over and looked at me with a long stare, not saying a word. He motioned toward me, hesitated momentarily, as if asking my permission, then kissed me so passionately that my body became limp and ached with desire. I knew from the first time I laid eyes on him at the pool that his juicy lips would not be a disappointment. I knew they would taste this good, feel this soft, control me this way. I wrapped my arms around him, gently stroking the nape of his neck with my fingers as we kissed, my head swirling with visions of things to come. We were oblivious to the driver's presence, but I would guess that this sort of thing happened all the time in carriages, being that they evoke such feelings of romanticism. I felt comfortable enough to let my hands slowly explore his body. I touched him and felt throbbing energy that I knew would later electrify me.

"Raven", Parker said in almost a whisper, "would you be with me tonight?"

I looked deeply into his eyes, then smiled calmly, knowing the feeling was mutual.

"My answer lies within my kiss."

I gently pulled his face toward mine and kissed him slowly and sensually.

"I want you." I said as more of a command than wishful thinking.

Parker sat up and told the driver to take us back to the Lounge so that we could get his car. I really don't remember the drive to Parker's house other than his warm hand stroking my thighs and my hand learning more about him. We didn't utter a word, but merely exchanged glances at one another and occasionally smiled. I felt totally secured being with him, and soon I was to feel the warmth and love of this beautiful Black man. The drive to his house seemed to take forever, and the wait was agony, but I knew that it would be well worth it.

The door to his townhouse opened and quickly closed once we were inside. Parker kissed my lips, then slid his lips freely across my face and up and down my neck. We began peeling our clothes off, letting them fall haphazardly to the floor. A red beam of light was broken as we crossed the threshold of the living room, and music began to fill the room.

"What an operator". I thought.

I didn't want to become just another conquest for him, just another fuck, but I wanted this man in my own selfish way for my own selfish purposes. TONIGHT! NOW!

"Parker, I hope you don't think that I do this with every..."

"Shush", Parker said, touching my lips with his index finger. "What I DO think, Ms. McNair, is that I'm gonna explode if I don't have you."

With Parker's finger still resting on my lips, I opened my mouth slightly, allowing it to slip into my mouth. I sucked it provocatively as he moved it to and fro, conjuring sexual images in both our minds. He removed his finger from my mouth and kissed me deeply, passionately.

Our bodies were a beautiful contrast; his complexion being jet black and mine a medium brown. Parker's build was firm and manly, an unbelievable sight that'll be forever etched in my mind. He had a broad chest that tapered down to a narrow waist. Effortlessly, Parker scooped me up and carried me near the fireplace where he lowered me down on the plush carpeting that covered the entire living room. I removed the rest of my clothing very slowly and seductively, dictating the pace of disclosure, but not Parker's eagerness. It was apparent that he longed for me. I tossed my teddy onto the floor to join the trail of the other garments.

"Damn baby!" Parker whispered. "You're beautiful."

I smiled, laying backwards onto the carpet. Parker leaned forward to connect his lips with my erect nipples. I sighed, feeling the warmth of his mouth surrounding them. He suckled them and licked them like he knew exactly how I wanted it to be done; squeezing them gently with his hand as if expecting milk, and nibbling intermittently with his teeth just so, but not to cause injury. My moans grew in intensity with the excitement of our act. With his free hand he placed it under my body, holding my ass. He then tucked both his hands up under me and slowly kissed his way down my chest, toward my stomach...

"Parker... baby... you're driving me crazy", I said smiling with satisfaction.

"Not yet baby. The pleasure's just beginning."

...over to my thigh, down my leg, then to the other leg, then kissed his way up that leg until he was where he wanted to be from the start. His face disappeared.

"Oh Parker, ahhhhhhhhh!" I gasped.

My body began moving at a much quickened pace as I rubbed the back of his head.

"Baby", I moaned, "this feels so damn good."

"It feels good to you baby?" Parker teased, momentarily raising his head to look at me.

"Yes, yes baby," I said emphatically, "it's so fucking good."

Parker's face disappeared again, my body moving in sync with his head. I cried out with pleasure, my back arched, my fingers penetrating firmly into his shoulders and his back. Damn, that was wonderful! I motioned for him to come up to where I was. He did. I turned him over on his back and straddled him.

"Baby you've got it comin' to you now". I said.

"Give it to me baby."

I leaned forward and kissed his lips. Before I leaned back, Parker's hands released the hairpin that held my French curl in place, allowing my hair to fall into his face. He ran his fingers through my hair. I felt Parker throbbing against my backside. I mounted him, giving him all the benefits of this position. Our breathing grew from controlled breaths to rapid, deep clutches of air.

Instinctively Parker knew all the right things to do for me. He knew when to do it and how much or how less of it to give. He was perfect.

"Is it all mine baby... is it mine?" Parker asked, looking very serious.

I nodded my head in agreement, not wanting to actually speak the words for fear that it'll all change in the morning. Besides, we often say things during the heat of passion that aren't necessarily fact, so I was reluctant to confirm any 'claims'.

"You're so beautiful Raven", Parker said.

I smiled, continuing my 'dance'. I lifted myself from him and positioned myself on my knees. Parker quickly followed and penetrated me, holding me close. His hands cupped my plump breast, then roamed downward holding onto my hips, enjoying its rhythmic motion. Parker's body began to move in a thunderous frenzy, pounding harder and deeper inside of me, holding me tighter to him with each thrust.

"Oh baby, this shit is serious! I'm gonna have to keep this all to myself", Parker whispered, barely able to speak coherently.

Parker shifted his 'gear' from one side to the other, then delivered firm and penetrating thrusts of authority.

"Parker… baby… shit." I said gasping. "You feel so damn good inside of me baby. You're gonna make me…"

"Make you what, baby?" Parker asked, now holding my cheeks in his hands and separating them.

"Make… me… make… me… ahhhhhhhhhhh!" I said, exploding in ecstasy.

"Oh yeah baby… yeah baby." Parker said. "Ahhhhhhhhhhhhhh!.

When Parker came, he let out a sound so animalistic that it almost frightened me, at least for the first time. We explored the other rooms of the house, engaging in a variety of sexual escapades, and in each room it got better than the time before. By 6 a.m., we had both collapsed, having fallen asleep in the bathtub. Prior to Parker, I considered myself pretty experienced; however that night taught me that all affairs that I'd had before him had been a waste of my time. He was everything I wanted in a lover; gentle and firm, patient and demanding, greedy and giving, nasty and gentlemanly, and very well endowed. Never had I been so thoroughly satisfied. I knew that beginning this night would be many more nights of passion, many more nights of ecstasy, and many more nights of fulfillment, but not anticipating the many long nights of sadness and solitude at the hands of one… Parker Whitfield.

Chapter 6:

Shortly after our first year of dating, I left Jerome's parents' home and moved in with Parker. We've managed to extend our first date into two years of dating. Jerome and I also extended our hiatus from the working world, the 'real' world. I sent out a few resumes, but to be totally honest, have not seriously pursued anything. For one reason or another, I'd not felt motivated. Jerome did, however, go on an interview that may in all likelihood land him a job in finance. Good for him.

I survived monetarily by using some of the money left to me from my parents' life insurance policy. Darlene's and my relationship has grown stronger as we've grown older. I consider her as not only my sister, but as my best friend. I love her dearly. She and I normally talk on the telephone a few times a week or so, although it has been nearly a month since we last spoke. I hadn't seen her since she, our brother Elliott, Aunt Sam, and Uncle Adam attended my Howard graduation three years ago. Darlene has grown to be a well-respected influential pillar of Iowa, becoming the youngest Editor-in-Chief in that region. She travels a great deal of the time on behalf of the Newspaper, attending conferences and conventions throughout the country. At thirty-one years old, Darlene has never been married, but has had a few serious relationships an countless marriage proposals. What man wouldn't want to catch hold of a beautiful, rising star?

"Darlene must be swamped with work at the Express because she hasn't called me in a while." I thought. "If I don't hear from her by the end of next week, I'll phone her to see what's going on."

One of my biggest fears is the thought of losing either Darlene or my brother Elliott. I don't know if I could bear that pain... again. Darlene finally called me mid-week, and I was relieved that she did.

"Hey baby sis! How's things going with you?"

"Pretty good", I said, "but I was becoming worried. Why haven't you called me?"

"I'm sorry sweetie." Darlene said. "There's been a lot of shit hitting the fan in the past few weeks. It's been unreal!"

"Like what?" I asked concerned.

"Like two bomb threats we received due to a story we ran exposing some local organized crime, like the multi-million dollar libel suit that's been waged against us from a councilman, like a staff writer I had to terminate because of improprieties..."

"Improprieties?"

"Yes, big time; he was being paid to suppress information on a public health story."

"Oh."

"Plus on top of all of this, I have to make some last-minute arrangements to the journalists convention in L.A."

"OK, ok," I interrupted, "I got the picture. Sorry for giving you shit."

Darlene laughed.

"Thanks sweetie," Darlene said.

I could tell by Darlene's voice that she was under a lot of stress.

"Are you going to be a speaker at the convention?" I asked eagerly.

"It looks that way, but I don't know. I've been trying to work out the details with the coordinator of the event for the last few days."

"That sounds exciting! Where in L.A. will it be held?"

"A new hotel that opened last year. It got major publicity because it was financed by one of those Savings and Loan crooks. I saw a picture of it in a magazine article and I must say that it is magnificent structure."

"Wow!" I said sounding like a 'baby' sister. "Congratulations."

"Don't congratulate me yet. I've also been given the green light to hire two new reporters that I know will be attending the conference. They are both very talented writers, and would be a great asset to the

Paper if I could get one of them, if not them both; So, while I'm there, I'll be trying to negotiate a deal on behalf of the Express."

"Well, good luck on that." I said. "If anyone can, I know that YOU can."

"Thanks baby. So, how's the love life going? You still happy with your musician guy? What's his name again… Parka? Windbreaker? " Darlene said laughing.

"Very funny Lois Lane", I said as I joined in her laughter. "Parker's his name, and yes I am very happy with him." I said proudly. "Maybe you and he can finally meet around Christmas if you aren't traveling or something."

"Well, I'll have to see." Darlene said.

Although Parker and Darlene had yet to meet, I told each about the other; Darlene about my talented, innovative, and sexy man, and told Parker about my courageous, intelligent, and highly independent big sister.

"I don't want to make you another promise like I did last year, then my travel plans change. I'll have to see what Gordon has in mind for the holidays and let you know, o.k.?"

"O.k., that sounds fair." I said, smiling already with the anticipation of seeing my sister. "So… you and Gordon are 'on' again, I take it?"

"Seems that way for now." Darlene said.

"You two break up and make up so often, I get confused."

"Yeah, me too sometimes, but we'll try it one more time. I think this will be 'it' for me if things don't work out. I'm really at the end of my rope with him."

"I heard that!" I said agreeing with her.

"It seems that we just can't agree on anything anymore. We argue over the smallest of situations; I really don't know why I'm still with him."

"You know why; you love the man."

"Is that it?" Darlene asked cynically. "I know that I used to. I'm not sure what you would call it now; fear… habit… security…" Darlene said. "Last week I decided that I needed a change, so I went to the salon and got my hair cut short, and dyed auburn. It looked really great."

"I bet you look stunning." I said.

"I do, if I must say so myself. As a mater of fact," Darlene continued, "in a strange sort of way, I look like that picture of Mom that Aunt Sam has in her photograph book of the two of them on vacation in Vermont." Darlene said.

"I know the picture very well." I said snickering. "I 'borrowed' it from Aunt Sam's photo book when I left Iowa. I carry it in my wallet all the time." I said smiling, thinking of how beautiful our mother was.

"Anyway, I then went to my ophthalmologist to pick up contacts that I'd been fitted for, turned in my glasses, and turned over a new attitude… at least until I got home. You would've thought that I'd murdered someone, by Gordon's reaction.

"Well, you know how men can be sometime." I said.

"Bullshit! This is MY life and MY body… not HIS." Darlene said in a perturbed manner. "That's a cop-out answer. Just like that other unacceptable saying, 'boys will be boys'. That shit doesn't work for me anymore. I'm just fed up with unnecessary bickering.

There was brief silence on the telephone from us both.

"Well anyway, I'll let you know something this weekend if I'm coming or not, ok? I miss you squirt." Darlene said.

"Me too", I responded, now feeling melancholy.

There was another moment of silence until Darlene interrupted and broke the somber mood.

"Anyway, how's that sweetheart of a guy Jerome Fleming doing? Are you two still, as you put it, 'bumming' around Atlanta together?"

"We were, until Rubenstein and Craft came along and put and end to it." I said somewhat disappointed. "Jerome now has a job with them, a major accounting firm here in Atlanta."

"Good for him! It's about time that you two get it in gear and act like adults. Tell him congrats for me".

"Ok. I will." I said obediently. "Between working full-time for Rubenstein and Craft, and juggling all of his women, there isn't much time left for he and I to see one another. Before he began working, we'd get together for drinks three or four times a week. Now, I'm lucky if we get together once a month!" I said.

"So, when are you going to…"

"I knew that you were going to bring that up again!" I snapped. "I'm working on it… sort of, but right now, I'm just relaxing."

"You've spent enough time relaxing, Raven." Darlene said, sounding like a mother. "Aunt Sam and Uncle Adam expects more of you than sitting around playing house. Hell, you should expect more of YOURSELF!"

I said nothing in response, knowing that Darlene was right. I knew that she was telling me these things for my own good.

"You're right." I said solemnly. "I'll do better."

"Ok baby. I love you. Take care of yourself and I'll talk to you as soon as I can, alright?"

"Alright. I love you too." I said, and hung up the phone.

I became very reflective after our conversation. Like Darlene, I also knew that I MUST make a change in my life, and soon.

Parker had spent almost a year creating new music at home in his recording studio. Soon after I moved in with him, he began touring with his band Sacga. He traveled at first in the surrounding region, then branched out further to perform concerts around the country. He still had his eye on the West Coast where he hoped to one day make it big with Saega. His agent had been working very hard on getting Parker the right exposure there, but so far nothing has panned out. I used to accompany him sometimes, but it became 'old' fast, as I didn't adjust well to life on the road. He had to be shared with his agent, the band, the road managers, the fans, and if there was anymore of him left, me. I suppose I became a bit jealous of jockeying for position. Silly, huh?

Parker finally got his chance to prove himself in LaLa land. His agent got Saega booked as the musical entertainment for a week-long engagement for the Harrison Hotel chain. Although it was a small job, Parker was ecstatic. He would be required to perform at a different Harrison hotel each night, seven hotels in all. Parker didn't particularly like this arrangement, but being that he wanted so badly to infiltrate this market, he accepted the job. Besides he'd been told by his agent that three out of the seven galas would have people of 'influence' from around the country in it's midst, so he couldn't beat this kind of exposure nor the free publicity which was certain to be generated from something like this. He felt that stardom for Saega was only a matter of time, and the clock was definitely ticking in his favor. The man was just that good... and confident. He asked me to accompany him, but I refused.

I knew he wouldn't have any time to spend with me, considering the band will have to move every night to another location. He promised, though, that he would call me everyday, and with the exception of one night, he did.

"Hi baby. How's my girl?"

"Fine baby, but missing you something awful."

"I miss you too."

"Well how did it go last night? Did you knock their socks off?" I asked.

"I sure did, although the night before had a much livelier crowd. This group was a bit 'stuffy'."

"Oh yeah? What group were they?" I asked.

"Last night's affair was sponsored by the Society of National and International Psychologists, so I think that they were afraid to let themselves go and enjoy themselves. They were probably all psychoanalyzing each other or watching for some Freudian behavior or something." Parker said chuckling. I laughed too.

"Meet anyone interesting? Made any connections?"

"Not at that joint, but tonight… you never know. I think my agent is putting some things together too. So, we'll see baby… we'll see. Hey, I've got to go now. I'll try calling you before the gig, but if I can't, I'll talk to you tomorrow, ok?"

"Sure baby. Play well and think of me." I said.

"I will baby, and I do." Parker said.

"Is that the way you're gonna say your marriage vows?" I asked facetiously.

"In due time girl, in due time. I've got to go." Parker said. "Goodbye baby. I love you."

"I love you too Parker."

On several occasions, Parker and I had broached the subject of marriage and having a family, but I could tell by his reaction that he wasn't ready for it and I never wanted to press him about it. I call it his triple 'A' defense… avoidance, annoyance, and attitude. Anyway, I felt that it WOULD one day happen, it was just a question of WHEN.

The Harrison's Chakassa Pavilion was enormous! The acoustics were ideal for musical performances and the design of the room, very elegant. Chandeliers hung above the marbled floor and ceiling-to-floor stained glass windows were positioned on either side of the room. The stage was constructed in the center of the floor, creating a theater-in-the-round setup, and the bar and buffet tables extended the full length of the wall.

"Damn Parker!" Will said. "Look at the size of this place. I feel like we're in the Taj Mahal, man!"

"It is beautiful", Rachel added, her eyes opened wide.

"Well, I say let's give them a reason to remember Saega. Let's give them the performance of our lives." Shanai chimed in.

"Yeah! That's basically what it comes down to." Ozzie said. "This tour could be the turning point that we need."

"You're right," added Butch. "This will determine how badly we want it. We can make it happen!"

"Well, let's get started." Parker commanded. "We've got about nine hours before show time. Let's set up, rehearse a little, then rest a bit."

The band members assisted the roadies in bringing the equipment in and setting it up: checking the mics, adjusting levels, and putting gels on various lights for effects. In essence, this will surely be a performance NOT to miss.

Chapter 7:

"Ms. McNair! Ms. McNair!"

Darlene turned around in the lobby of the hotel to witness two women approaching her, half running.

"Ms. McNair, I'm glad we caught you." they said almost out of breath. "We just wanted to say that we thoroughly enjoyed your speech on Minority Women in Print Media. My name is Tahira Richardson".

The young woman extended her hand toward Darlene. She reciprocated.

"And this is my friend and colleague JoJo White.."

Darlene shook her hand as well.

"How do you do ladies?" Darlene said.

"We're with the Baltimore Bulletin. You've been an inspiration to me since I read about you in Jet Magazine when you were a reporter for the "Express". Tahira added.

"And, of course now that you're the Editor-in-Chief… it's just so impressive!" JoJo said with enthusiasm.

"Thank you very much ladies. I'm flattered." Darlene said smiling. "I really do appreciate your appreciation.".

"Can we buy you a drink Ms. McNair? We were on our way into the lounge when we saw you." Tahira offered sincerely.

"No, no thanks. I'm a bit exhausted from the pace of the convention events. I think I'll just catch a quick nap before the evening's ball. Will you be there tonight?"

"Oh yes, we wouldn't miss it for the world." Tahira said. "Besides, it's already paid for by the Bulletin, so we'll be there."

"Great, then I'll see you both tonight." Darlene said as she began to walk away.

"Thanks Ms. McNair." They both said.

"No, thank you ladies, and good luck in your careers."

Darlene walked to her suite feeling that her trip had become a success. She had contributed in lighting a fire of inspiration in the hearts of two young people. She took off her suit, turned on the radio, and laid across the bed, thinking about her future with Gordon and how lonely she feels. She reached over for the telephone and called him, catching up on things at home and to fill him in on her developments in L.A. She got off of the telephone after having yet another tense conversation with him, and fixed herself a drink to try to ease the pounding in her head. She wished for the happier times that they'd shared a year ago, before their troubles began. She had doubts before on whether they would be able to survive, and time is proving that her doubts were indeed justified. No longer did she dream of marriage with Gordon, just companionship, just a warm body. She hated the fact that she 'lowered her bar' and settled for an unfulfilled relationship. She resumed laying down on the bed and soon drifted off to sleep. When Darlene awoke, it was 8:15p.m. She sprang from the bed in a panic.

"Shit!" she said, upset that she didn't set her clock to wake her.

She jumped into the shower, and dressed herself at brake-neck speed. By 9p.m., she was all ready to go. Fortunately enough for her, the event was in the same hotel.

The seating arrangements were predetermined and she knew beforehand that she'd be seated at table number 33, with several of her old media pals.

"Darlene, Darlene! Over here!" a voice called out.

Darlene looked in the direction of the voice and smiled, recognizing her friends seated at a circular table.

"Good to see you girl! We weren't sure if you were going to make it tonight or not". Melissa said.

"Yeah, I overslept a little. Why didn't you ring my room?"

"I told you so", Theresa burst out. "I told her, Darlene, that we should call you, but nooo!"

"Shut up Theresa!" Melissa retorted.

"No, you shut up! You're not ALWAYS right, you know!" Theresa said, in such a loud voice that it attracted the attention of several guests seated at the surrounding tables.

"Ladies, ladies, calm down. I'm here now, right?" Darlene said laughing as she took her seat. "You two haven't changed one bit. You're still the dueling sisters of the Globe." Darlene said as she hugged them both.

"Darlene, how did the workshop go this morning?" Michael asked.

"Things went well. I was very happy with the enthusiasm from the attendees. I think there's still a lot of untapped talent out there." Darlene said.

I agree with you on that." Karen said.

At that moment, Darlene spotted one of the two reporters that she wanted to talk to about working for her newspaper.

"Hold that thought Karen. I've gotta make a connection."

"With whom?" Karen asked, turning around to try and track Darlene's line of sight.

"Can't say right now. I'll be right back."

And with that, Darlene excused herself from the table and walked over to table number 17, where she approached the reporter and conducted a pseudo business meeting and interview right there on the spot. When she left the reporter, Darlene was smiling, the reporter was smiling, and the 'Express' had obtained a new reporter on it's staff, at least verbally. Next week, the Express will fly him to Iowa to discuss and solidify the deal.

Everyone had already eaten from the well-stocked buffet table by the time Darlene arrived, however food was still available. Ann and Karen accompanied her to the buffet table as she prepared her plate. After eating, Darlene joined everyone else in networking and mingling until the entertainment began.

"Ladies and gentlemen", a voice was heard over the loudspeaker, "it is the Harrison Hotel's distinct privilege to introduce to you tonight's musical guests. On behalf of the Society of Journalists, Incorporated, I present to you... Saega!"

Everyone applauded as the lights slowly dimmed to black, leaving the entire crowd in darkness. The band, dressed in black tails, was already positioned on the platform. The drummer, Will, hit the drumsticks together and counted off "one, two, one, two, three, four". The spotlight shone on Saega and the band came alive. After a few bars, the lights cut off again very abruptly. Parker, dressed in white tails, made his entrance with a single red spotlight on him as he walked down the center aisle toward the stage playing a sax solo. Everyone applauded wildly, as Parker and the band had the audience mesmerized. After about an hour of music, there was a twenty-minute intermission, whereby the networking and chatter resumed.

"We should invite him over for a drink at our table." Ann said, looking toward Parker.

"Leave the man alone," Darlene said. "Didn't Larry accompany you here?"

"You wouldn't know it to look at him." Ann said as she looked in Larry's direction as he sat at another table laughing and entertaining three beautiful women.

"Oh, so you want to get back at Larry by inviting 'Mr. Music' over, huh?" asked Joel.

"No, not at all." denied Ann, with a questionable smile. "I'm just trying to be courteous... friendly... hospitable."

Everyone at the table laughed. Ann got the attention of one of the waiters and had him deliver a message to Parker to join their table for a drink. As Parker walked toward the table, he received congratulatory pats on the back and handshakes for his performance. Parker was loving every moment of this, because it puts him one step closer to his dream of success with Saega. Joel suddenly rose from the table.

"I can't sit here and be a party to this 'attack' on this poor man that I'm SURE's coming." Joel said smiling to all of the ladies at the table.

He bent down and kissed Melissa on the lips lightly.

"I'll return when intermission's over darling."

Melissa nodded her head in agreement. As Parker neared their table, he noticed that table number 33 consisted of five beautiful women: a blond, two brunettes, one auburn haired, and one brown haired.

Although Michael was also seated, his presence did not register at all with Parker until the introductions.

"Hello ladies... and gentleman." Parker said, nodding his head toward the specified gender and making direct eye contact with everyone. "Thanks for your invitation."

"It's our pleasure. Please have a seat and make yourself comfortable." Ann said.

Parker did as he was told. Everyone introduced themselves on a first name basis, and he responded in kind, using his nickname Cozy.

"You play wonderfully." Ann commented.

"You certainly do." Theresa added. "How long have you been playing Cozy?"

"Since I was a child," Parker said, "but as a young man, I toured with CJ London's band for a few years. I guess that's where I really established my style."

"Well, thank GOD for CJ London", Ann said, "because I love your... your style."

Embarrassed by Ann's unsubtleness, everyone smiled and exchanged looks at each other.

"So", Darlene said, "is Cozy your real name or stage name?"

"And are you married?" Ann forcefully asked.

"Ok, that one did it for me!" Michael said interrupting. "Young man, I stayed as long as I could to give you some male support over here, but I see that you're surrounded by barracudas. You're on your own, son."

Michael slapped Parker on his back, as if saying goodbye to a comrade going off to war. Everyone was laughing as they ordered another round of drinks.

"Hey Ann," there's Bernard Law from the Kilgore Press Magazine over there." Melissa said, trying to distract her from her obvious mission of enticing Parker.

"Where, where?" Theresa said. I haven't talked to him since our last convention in Texas."

"That is just like my sister, to 'not get it'" Melissa whispered to Darlene. They both laughed.

Parker, looking at Darlene, felt something familiar about Darlene, something in her smile, in her eyes. He felt that he'd seen her somewhere before, but didn't know how to bring it up at the table without sounding like he was trying to pick her up.

"I'm not interested in talking to boring Bernard". Ann. said without taking her eyes off of Parker. "I've got more urgent NEEDS, if you know what I mean." She licked her lips slowly and pursed them as if kissing Parker.

"Boring Bernard? Are you kidding? The man won a Pulitzer, for goodness sake! Intelligent, powerful, talented, friendly, but never can he be called 'boring'". Karen said. "I'm going over for a few. I'll be back later." She said to everyone at the table.

"Me too." Theresa said.

"I think I'd like to say hello to him too." Melissa said. She arose from the table, along with Karen and Theresa. As she lifted herself up, she bent over and whispered in Darlene's ear.

"Ann's going to make a fool of herself. She's had way too much to drink. I'm going to get Larry from the other table to come over and get her. Stay here with her to make sure she doesn't take things too far, ok?"

"Ok." Darlene agreed.

Watching the three women abandon her with inebriated Ann, Darlene tried to make general small talk with Parker, but Ann would not here of it. She continued to sway the conversation towards sex, specifically between her and Parker, and even kicked her shoes off, to what Darlene presumed was to play 'footsie' with him under the table. Larry arrived at the table just in time and escorted Ann to the other side of the room, giving her the excuse that he wanted to talk to her about their relationship… in private.

"Is your friend always this shy?" Parker said laughing.

Darlene joined in the laughter.

"I apologize for Ann. She's really a lovely woman. She just had a bit too much to drink."

"No problem. I didn't take any offense to her behavior, but thanks for the apology anyway." Parker said.

They both smiled a pleasant smile at one another and once again Parker was struck with the feeling that he'd seen Darlene before. Darlene, on the other hand, couldn't help but notice Parker's beautiful smile, revealing his pearly white teeth. She looked beyond his ruffled shirt and imagined his broad chest: kinky hair? Straight hair? No hair? Then looked back at his face, thinking it doesn't matter if he has hair on his chest or not. The man was HOT! She also noticed that he was not wearing a ring on his finger.

"Unattached and available, the perfect combination." she thought.

"I hope that you don't take this to be a 'come-on' line, but I feel that we've met somewhere before. Do I look familiar to you?" Parker asked.

"Here we go!" Darlene said smiling. "Men are men where ever you go. Is that the best you could come up with?"

"No, no, I really mean it! Your face is very familiar to me for some reason."

"Well, I'm positive that I've never met you before. Had I, I would've remembered." Darlene said smiling.

"Thank you for the compliment." Parker said.

"That wasn't a compliment to you. That was a compliment to my great memory." Darlene said.

They both laughed.

"Excuse me, but it's time man." Butch said to Parker as he neared the table.

"Well, it's show time. Maybe we can talk after the show?" Parker asked.

"Maybe." Darlene said smiling a warm smile, knowing that she would wait until the end of the performance, and knowing that she wouldn't mind being held in his arms. Darlene longed to feel the comforting caress of a man. The tension that exists between her and Gordon has made her life insufferable.

Parker and the band returned to the stage and gave a solid performance, finishing around 1a.m. the crowd, however, was still in a festive mood, and spilled out into the streets of L.A. in search of other celebrations. Some remained at the Pavilion chatting, while still others called it a night and returned to their hotel rooms. Parker sought Darlene after the performance and invited her to a nightcap in his room. She refused, but did agree to a drink with him in the hotel's lounge.

The bar was very crowded, with a sizeable number of it's patrons trickling in from the Pavilion. The overhead music played mostly R&B.

Parker and Darlene ordered drinks from the bar, then made their way to one of the few spaces that wasn't occupied; a cramped corner where they stood near the kitchen, nursing their drinks.

"So Darlene", Parker said, "you pretty much have an indication of what I do for a living, tell me about yourself? You must be in the media, being that you're here at this convention. What is it that you do?"

"I'm the Editor of a newspaper". Darlene said.

"Iowa?" Parker said with surprise. "You're the second person that I've met in my entire life from Iowa. Before her, I really didn't think that there WERE black folk in the corn fields of the Midwest."

"Why sir, I do believe that you're in need of a little education then." Darlene said jokingly in a southern accent. "Just goes to show how much you don't know."

"O.K. You got me." Parker said smiling. "But really Darlene", he continued, "what are you doing in Iowa? How did you end up there?"

"It's a long story Cozy. I don't want to waste your time hearing about that." Darlene said, dismissing the inquiry. "However, a more immediate question is what are we doing HERE... what is THIS all about?" Darlene asked as she moved her finger around the brim of her glass suggestively.

She looked directly at him, her eyes shifting between his eyes and his lips hungrily, hoping that this night can fill at least one of the voids that she has in her life. Parker looked at her and smiled a confident smile.

"You're being naughty". he said pointing his finger at her, shaking it.

"I know. Are you suggesting that I stop?"

Parker smiled.

"Oh no, not in the least. I rather like it... very much."

Parker and Darlene smiled at one another in silence. Then feeling the frustration again of not being able to place her face.

"I feel that I know you from somewhere Darlene, I just can't put my finger on it."

"I've got a better idea of where you can put your finger. Let me see if I can help you."

Darlene reached for Parker's hand and put it around her waist. Then she began moving to the music ever so slightly. Ironically 'If Only For One Night' by Luther Vandross was playing.

"What are you trying to do to me lady?" Parker asked rhetorically, feeling the contour of her body with her syncopated motion. "I now understand why you're in the media; you're a very persuasive communicator."

"But can you deal with my message?" Darlene asked.

"Well, personally, I think that the message may require further study, you know, a deeper, more thorough examination. Would that be agreeable to you?"

Darlene smiled a wicked smile that anyone looking at her face would immediately know the subject matter of their conversation.

"I would love to receive a deeper probe". Darlene said whispering in his ear.

"Your eyes, your smile..." Parker's eyes continued downward, looking at her voluptuous body then back up to her face. "I know that I know you, don't I?" he said, now second-guessing himself. "Was it Morgan State University?"

"No, I've never been there." Darlene replied.

"What about seeing the CJ London band perform? Have you ever been to a concert featuring the band?" Parker asked, still reaching for answers.

"I've heard of the band of course, but no, I've never been to a concert. Guess you'll have to try again, Sherlock."

Parker was completely baffled. It wasn't very often that his memory would not come through for him.

"Well, I'm sure it'll come to you sooner or later." Darlene said, not knowing just how true her words would become.

They talked and laughed till 2:30a.m. By now they'd obtained a table, as the crowd was thinning out. The bartender announced that the bar would be closing in fifteen minutes, so they decided to have 'one more for the road', already knowing where their road would lead them.

"Wait a second," Darlene said, trying to help Parker with the mystery, "have you ever visited Iowa?"

"You've got to be kidding?" Parker said sarcastically. For what reason would I visit Iowa?"

"I don't know, perhaps to visit your wife and kids?" Darlene said, 'fishing'.

They both smiled.

"If that's your way of asking me whether or not I'm married, the answer is no, I'm not, nor do I have any children, although I'd like to someday."

"So why isn't there a woman in your life? An attractive man like yourself shouldn't be all alone out here in this great, big, world." Darlene said. "Is it that you prefer men?"

"Again, wrong." Parker said smiling, enjoying Darlene's directness and playfulness. "I didn't say that there was no woman in my life. I said that I wasn't married."

"Well, if you have a girlfriend Cozy, then why are you here with me?"

"Other than the fact that I find you very attractive, Darlene, there's something intriguing about you, something familiar, yet unknown."

They stared into each other's eyes. Parker leaned forward and kissed Darlene gently on her lips. As he pulled back, he looked into her eyes again, she smiled, and before she could say a word, he again advanced forward kissing her, placing another gentle kiss on her lips.

"You have a very sweet set of lips." Darlene said.

"Maybe before you leave L.A., you'll give me the pleasure to tell you the exact same thing." Parker said.

The chemistry between them was undeniable. Parker touched Darlene's hand, which was resting on the table, then slowly moved his hand upwards on her arm. Darlene felt herself becoming weak to his touch.

"Mmm, that feels good, very relaxing." Darlene said.

"Are you ready to go?" Parker asked.

"Yes, but I think I'd prefer my suite, if you don't mind.".

"I don't mind at all".

Parker left money on the table to more than cover their tab, and held Darlene's hand as he led her out of the lounge. They entered the door leading to the hotel's lobby and boarded an empty elevator. Parker put his hand across the elevator door, preventing it's closing.

"You sure you want this?" Parker asked.

"What specifically are you asking Parker... just to be sure that we fully understand one another?"

"You... for tonight... with no strings... no commitments... no promises... no regrets."

"In other words, you simply want to fuck me? Is that right?" Darlene asked bluntly with a serious look on her face that could easily be interpreted as outrage.

Parker looked directly into her eyes without smiling, taking a chance with his answer of possibly insulting her.

"Yes, unequivocally yes."

"Well, in that case, I think that we understand one another just fine." Darlene said, now smiling again.

Parker smiled as well. He removed his hand from the door and the elevator took them to the twenty-third floor to Darlene's suite. The music on the radio was still playing low from when Darlene was napping earlier. She requested that they take a shower, to which Parker was more than happy to oblige. He loved Darlene's curvaceous body, lathering it all over with soap. He thought it so erotic seeing the water from the shower head stream through her hair, down her face, washing away the suds from her full breasts, down toward her stomach. Darlene, too, enjoyed seeing... enjoyed touching Parker, and happy to be a contributing part of the metamorphosis that was taking place with his body. She turned around facing the shower head while Parker was positioned behind her.

"Damn, is this the way they grow 'em in Iowa?" Parker said quite pleased with Darlene's ass.

"Baby, Iowa is known for growing a lot of things, but I don't think they are in the business of planting, picking, or producing ass." Darlene said laughing.

"Well, all I know is that we'd better get out of here now before I CAN'T get out of here."

Parker put both of his hands to either side of her waist. Darlene smiled, turned around and kissed him passionately while the water hit her back. Parker picked her up with her legs wrapped around him, threw back the shower curtain, and walked into the bedroom as they continued kissing.

"You know there's no backing out now baby." Parker said.

"What makes you think that I would want to. I want this as much as you do". Darlene responded. "Maybe more."

Parker gently laid Darlene back onto the bed.

"Wait one second angel while I get my wallet." Parker said, feeling a degree of responsibility in the midst of his lust. "Like I told you before, I don't want any regrets. I'll be right back."

"Hurry back lover."

He walked to the other side of the room to get his pants that, in his haste to join Darlene in the shower, lay draped over a suitcase. He lifted his pants and removed several packets from his wallet. As he was returning his pants onto the suitcase, his eyes caught a glimpse of the name tag that was attached to the handle. Parker, not believing what he 'thinks' he saw, bent down toward the suitcase to get a closer look.

"Darlene McNair? Iowa?" he mumbled. "Oh no, this can't be! Of all people… Raven's sister? Shit! That's where I know her face from!"

This now jars Parker's memory to a photograph in Raven's wallet of her mother as a young woman. With Darlene's new hair image, she bore an uncanny resemblance to a very young Mrs. McNair.

"What's taking you so long, baby? Have you changed your mind?"

"I'm… I'm on my way." Parker said, his head swirling with confusion.

"What are you doing baby, trying them out?" Darlene said jokingly.

He was about to turn to go back to her, but suddenly she was behind him, wrapping her arms around him, allowing her hands to massage his penis.

"I got lonely over there all by myself. You having some trouble over here?"

"Look, Darlene…"

He turned around to face her, his chest beating hard and fast, his mouth dry, and his head spinning like a top.

"Darlene, wait. I think that we should talk."

"Talk?" Darlene whispered as she kissed his neck. "I just hope that you're as long lasting as you are long winded."

"Baby, you're making this harder for me to…"

"Isn't that the whole idea, lover?" Darlene said, now kissing his chest and making her way downward.

"Darlene, listen to me." Parker said in a more stern voice.

He placed his hands on both of Darlene's arms. At that moment, Darlene knelt down, connecting her mouth with his penis.

"Oh God." Parker whispered, dropping the rubbers to the floor.

Parker lifted her from the floor and carried her to the bed a few feet away. He proceeded to give her what she'd been craving, what she'd been missing in her relationship with Gordon: passion, excitement, spontaneity, happiness and most importantly good lovin'. Parker thought back to his telephone conversation with Raven yesterday: 'play well and think of me', she said. Well, he did and he was. He thought of how he's jeopardizing his future with Raven, the woman he swore to that his life with other women was over. That she would be the only one that he made love to. His guilt-plagued mind was telling him that what he was doing was wrong, that this is unforgivable, that this is suicide! Darlene was all over him, like a love-starved fiend. She began to make Parker feel comfortable enough to let down his resistance.

"God help me…" Parker thought as he entered Darlene again. "God help my weak, black ass."

From that moment, she became his to enjoy and love, till the break of dawn.

Chapter 8:

Darlene called the next morning. She told me that the convention was indeed a success even though she didn't get to talk to the other reporter that she wanted signed to the Express. She received a lot of positive feedback from the workshop she chaired, and the convention coordinator has invited her to be among twenty-five representatives from the United States to attend a Spring conference in Europe next year. I told her of my renewed employment drive, to which she was ecstatic. She offered her services of putting me in touch with some of her personal contacts in the legal profession, but I declined her offer… at least for now. I want to see how far I can take it on my own, without anyone's influence or intervention. She told me that all she had to do was to make a few phone calls and she was certain that she could find me something, but again I refused her.

"I'm proud of you Raven, and never forget that I'm in your corner… always!" Darlene said sincerely.

"Thank you Lene. Hey", I said wanting to now change the subject, "how's things progressing with Gordon? Has he warmed up to your new look yet?" I asked.

"Gordon?" she said, as though it was a forbidden word. "So much has happened since I've returned home baby sis. My new look is the least of issues at this time."

"Oh?" I asked.

"Oh yeah!" Darlene said with a spark of excitement in her voice. "Gordon and I have split up for good this time, and surprisingly enough, I didn't feel anything like I thought I would feel. I wasn't sad, I wasn't angry, or even confused. It was more like a relief to my system. I felt nothing but joy and exhilaration with the thought of moving on with my life, free of Gordon and his baggage." Darlene said.

"Sounds as though you needed to make that move a lot sooner if it's had this kind of positive effect on you."

"No shit! I can't begin to put into words the weight that lifted off of my shoulders!"

"Well, as long as you're happy, so am I." I said.

"Sweetheart, I am more than happy. I feel... ALIVE!"

Darlene was undoubtedly a different person. A happy person. I'd not heard her sound this way since she and Gordon started dating a few years ago.

"Raven... darling... there's more." Darlene said in a child-like, playful voice.

"I'm listening." I said hesitantly.

"I've already begun dating this wonderful man from Chicago. Can you believe it?" she said excited.

"You're not wasting any time, are you babe?"

"Unfortunately I've wasted enough time with Gordon, but no more of that shit for me."

Darlene went on to tell me that her new guy, Novelle Colbert, is an entertainment lawyer. He represented the newly signed reporter, from the L.A. trip, and negotiated his contract with the Express.

"You know Raven, I always felt that there was someone out there for me. Someone that I can make plans with on sharing my future."

"I've never heard you sound so... so..."

"So logical?" Darlene interrupted.

"Yeah, that too." I said.

"I knew that Gordon wasn't the 'one', yet I stayed. I even hooked up with a total stranger while in L.A., but like the song goes, I was merely looking for love in all the wrong places."

"Excuse me? What was that?" I asked, not believing what I'd heard.

"You heard me right." She said as I felt her smiling through the telephone. "I spent my last night there in the arms of a stranger. It was very nice."

"The convention or the lovin'?" I asked jokingly.

"The convention of course."

We both laughed.

"The lovin'", she continued, "was unforgettable. I've never had an intimate experience like that ever! The man was a God-send, albeit temporary."

"Well maybe you should've held onto him a little while longer if he was 'all that'". I said. "You know, a good man is awfully hard to find these days."

"And a hard man is ALWAYS a good find." Darlene resplied.

We both laughed again.

"Well, with Novelle, I don't have that to worry about anymore.

"Great! But wait a second; back up a bit. I want to hear about this West Coast fling." I said. "Since when do you skip over details."

"I'll fill you in when I get there during the Christmas holidays."

"So you're coming? You're really coming this year?"

"Yes baby, I'll be there for sure this year." Darlene said.

"Bet. Will Novelle be coming with you?" I asked.

"He always does," Darlene said, as we both were thinking naughty thoughts.

We laughed.

"…but yes he will be joining me."

"Good! I'll invite Jerome and a few other friends over and make a big celebration out of it. Is that fine with you?"

"Sure, that's just fine. I can't wait to meet your Parka, or Eddie Bauer." Darlene said jokingly.

"That's 'Parker', missy." I joked back. "But Darlene, Parker has a commitment in L.A. during Christmas."

"Oh no!" Darlene said. "I'm never gonna meet this guy!"

"Well, we can always try again for something in the spring." I said.

"No we can't. Remember Sis, I'm going to Europe."

"Shit! We'll figure out something. Let's just say that you'll meet him next time." I said.

"Sure baby, maybe next time."

"Merry Christmas!"

Darlene and I shouted to one another as I opened the door, welcoming my rain-soaked sister and her boyfriend into my home. We hugged each other in a strong embrace and kissed on the cheek, laughing all the while. We were both so happy to finally be in the comfort of each other's arms; to be held by family.

"Raven, this is my friend Novelle, and baby," she said looking toward Novelle, "this is my beautiful sister Raven."

"Please Raven, call me Rock, all of my friends do." Novelle said as he extended his hand.

"Come here you!" I said pushing Novelle's hand away, hugging him. "I was beginning to doubt whether you were for real or not."

"Oh, he's for real alright." Darlene said smiling radiantly.

"Well, I've heard nothing but good things about you. Keep it up." I said.

"You can count on it." Novelle said with conviction as he helped Darlene take off her coat.

"Come on in and meet everyone."

I led them into the living room. Jerome saw Darlene enter the room and tore himself away from the circle of friends he'd been chatting with.

"Darlene! Hey baby." Jerome yelled.

"Rome! Boy, you haven't changed one bit." Darlene said as they hugged.

"Like I always say, why tamper with perfection." Jerome replied.

They laughed. Although it was never formally verbalized, we considered Jerome as family, as our brother. Jerome introduced himself to Novelle and took them around to meet everyone else at the party while I continued helping Sarah and Phyllis prepare the food in the kitchen. We had turkey, sweet potatoes, string beans, baked beans, cranberry sauce, mashed potatoes with gravy, rolls, collard greens, honey-baked ham, and for dessert, homemade peach and apple cobbler, pound cake and assorted ice cream. To drink? Iced tea and enough alcoholic beverages to open our own brewery. Nearly twenty people showed up, some were friends, others were friends of friends, while still others were strangers that I was meeting for the first time. But, it really didn't matter though. After all, this is the season for giving, is it not? Besides, I was feeling very lonely. With Parker being away, I figured that the more people I had surrounding me, the less alone I'd feel. Well, at least it sounded good.

Jerome brought his new lady love, Cheryl. Mitch and the now very pregnant Anita were there, Sheila and two of her out-of-town cousins were there, Sarah and Phyllis, two waitresses from The White Dove Lounge, along with their dates, Delores and her new beau Thomas, Jerome's parents, Trent and three questionable women that, to this day, I'm not sure where he picked them up from, and last but surely not least, Darlene and Novelle. During dinner, we played festive Christmas music. The atmosphere was very warm and everyone seemed to be having a wonderful time. People were dancing, playing board games, playing Wii games, playing cards, and watching endless football games on the wide screen tv; just enjoying themselves! There was constant activity all around the house. I like that. The rain continued to fall outside and at one point, our lights flickered, as there was now thunder and lightning that accompanied the downpour. I decided, before I became too comfortable, or lazy, that I'd load the dishwasher and clear the dinner table. Darlene volunteered to help me, and who am I to argue with her. We were busily putting dishes away when we resumed our earlier telephone conversation about her L.A. trip. She told me that they'd gone for drinks after the gala, that they agreed to go to her room when the bar closed, and that his sexual prowess was both romantic and erotic.

"I must admit, I did feel somewhat guilty about cheating on Gordon at first but by the time we'd entered my suite, it was like, 'Gordon who?'" Darlene said.

We laughed.

"Have you heard from him since?" I asked.

"No, but I wasn't expecting that to happen either. We both knew that this was a one night, one time deal."

She went on to say that they made love till about five or six a.m. and described, in great detail, the various positions they performed, beaming with delight.

"How exciting". I said.

"And it was." Darlene said.

"Did you find enough time between humping to at least ask him his name?"

"Sort of. I never got his real name?"

"What?" I said in disbelief. "You've spent an intimate night with a guy and don't even know his name? This sounds so unlike you. I'm stunned, sis."

"Wait a second now! You make it sound a lot worse than it was. He did mention a name to me... Cozy? Comfy?..."

"Cozy?" I said, thinking that this was too much of a coincidence: Darlene's lover goes by the name of Cozy, same as Parker; that he plays the saxophone, as does Parker; that he was in L.A. during the same time frame as was Parker. Too many coincidences, damnit! My heart started beating very rapidly. I turned my back to Darlene to supposedly put away the condiments into the cabinet, but in reality I wanted to hide my face from her because I knew that it reflected my fear. I had to pursue one more question, for my own confirmation. Could this man, this bastard, be one and the same?

"Darlene, do you know the name of his band?" I asked as my voice quivered a bit.

"It was something like Santa... no that wasn't it... maybe say... say..." Darlene struggled.

"Saega?" I said, still with my back to her.

"Yeah, yeah, that's it! How did you know that?" Darlene asked, impressed with my guess.

"Oh, I've heard of the group before. They're pretty well-known." I said, my eyes swelling with tears then closing in pain. My heart was broken.

"Darlene, can you come here for a minute honey?" Novelle called out to her from the basement.

"O.K. baby." Darlene yelled back.

She hit me playfully with a dishtowel that she had draped over her shoulders.

"I'll be right back baby."

She walked out of the kitchen, and I walked out shortly behind her and out of the house into the pouring rain. I couldn't bear to face her again, so soon after hearing that she 'fucked' my boyfriend. I couldn't pretend that it didn't happen, that she didn't say it. It wasn't that I was angry with her so much as it was the betrayal I feel toward Parker. Had it not been Darlene, it would've been someone else... with me probably

NEVER finding out. This is just one that has backfired in his face, the bastard! My head was so clouded that I didn't even stop to get a coat or an umbrella to protect myself from the elements. I was in shock!

I walked across the street to an open area that the neighborhood uses as a softball field, my arms wrapped around myself. I was sobbing uncontrollably now, totally oblivious to activity around me. Nothing mattered anymore between Parker and I. I felt like I was a shattered woman; with every question that I asked Darlene, another piece of my heart shattered. I walked from one end of the field to the other and back again, over and over again, thinking of the warning that Jerome had given me when I first met Parker at the YMCA. I began to question everything; the time that he's spent away from me when he's on the road; was this the activity that was going on? My trust in him is broken FOREVER!

I now wished that I didn't have a houseful of people inside my home. I just wanted to be alone to deal with my hurt. I was now at the farthest end of the field. I turned around and looked in the direction of my house. Jerome was running toward me carrying an umbrella and a coat. When he reached me, he was surprised to see my face in such pain. He put the coat around my shoulders and held the umbrella over our heads.

"So, what's this all about doll?" he asked, as he walked with me for another 'spin' around the field. In telling him, I stopped and cried on his shoulders while we hugged. He wasn't too shocked to hear that it involved Parker and another woman, but he was totally caught off guard to hear that the other woman was Darlene.

"What? I'm gonna kill him." Jerome angrily said.

"No Rome, death would be too easy a punishment for him." I replied.

I explained to Jerome that Darlene is unaware that Cozy and Parker are one and the same. I wanted to believe that Darlene had to have been an innocent party from the way in which she told it to me, without holding back details. I know that she wouldn't deliberately hurt me this way, our love and respect for one another is far stronger than that. If I can help it, I don't want her to ever find out the truth about this nightmare. This would devastate her. Jerome said that Darlene returned upstairs to the kitchen to find me gone, and called him to ask him where I might be.

"I just happened to look out of the window, and here you are!" Jerome said, still hugging me with one arm and holding the umbrella with the other hand, as we continued walking.

"What am I gonna do Rome?" I asked, in need of his advice.

"Well, you damn sure aren't gonna stay here! You don't deserve that kind of disrespect."

"What am I gonna tell Darlene was the reason why I left the house the way that I did?" I asked again, unable to think straight.

"Tell her… tell her you felt ill, no… tell her that you were thinking about your parents and became sad, no… tell her…"

"That's o.k. Rome. I'll think of something. Thanks anyway."

I'd been walking in the rain for nearly thirty minutes. I was now aware that the weather was kind of chilly and was glad that Jerome brought me my coat. He convinced me that we should return to the house. I guess it appeared very strange for us to be walking around in the rain with guests inside the house. As we made our way back to the house, I felt very numb, somber; as though I was leaving a cemetery… or a funeral. In a sense, I was.

When I returned inside, none of the guests even missed me: the women were still chatting, the men were totally immersed in the football game, and the Christmas music still filled the house. I was happy in that I had not ruined the other's good time and was not the center of attention. Darlene, however, was filled with questions, wanting to know what happened to me. Why did I leave the house? Why had I been crying? Feeling a loss for an explanation, I used one of the suggestions that Jerome had mentioned and told her that I'd been thinking of our parents and how much I missed them. She embraced me in her arms. I began to cry again, which in turn made her cry. Of course everyone knows that the holidays can have a joyous as well as depressing effect on people, so quite naturally that explanation was immediately accepted without question. For me, the only questions that I had could only be answered by one; again, Parker.

Darlene's stay was only for three days, the first of which was now gone. For the remaining days, we crammed in as many things as we could. We went clothes shopping, visited an art museum, took in a movie matinee, and visited Jerome's parents for a brief introduction. Before I knew it, the time had come for my sister to leave me. We've always had very emotional good-byes, but carrying around the additional knowledge of the affair made our usual tearful goodbye even more so. During my drive home, I couldn't help but reflect on the situation between Darlene and Parker, and vowed again to myself that Darlene is never to know the truth; that this would be information that I'll take to my grave. I held so much promise on a future with Parker that I never gave any consideration before to such a predicament as this. I thought that, yes, we would one day marry and have a family; but now those thoughts seem to have been nothing but the silly fantasies of a young woman in love. Once again Parker has forced me into a world I'd not prepared for. This time instead of forcing me to grow up, he's motivated me to wake up; wake up and take control of my life. Thanks Parker.

Chapter 9:

I arrived back home for what would be the last time. I'd made arrangements with Jerome's parents to return to their home tomorrow afternoon and stay in the room that I used to occupy when Jerome and I returned from Howard University. Coincidentally, on this same day, Parker will return from the road. I loaded a pile of clothes into the washing machine, thinking that I'd, at least, arrive at the Cunningham's with clean clothes. I grabbed a bottle of wine from the bar and took it with me to the laundry room, where I planned to drown my sorrows and sulk. As the wine flowed, so did my tears. So much so that my face had now become puffy and red. I'd finished better than half of the bottle when a burst of anger swelled up inside of me. I suddenly stopped feeling sorry for myself and started despising him... hating him even!

"What in the fuck have I done to deserve this shit?" I asked myself aloud. "Not one damn thing!" I answered. "Who the fuck does he think he is to just shit on me this way, the sneaky, whorish bastard! And fucking my own SISTER?"

The more I thought about it, the angrier I became; the angrier I became, the more I drank; the more I drank, the more vindictive and devious my thoughts grew. Never before had the saying 'hell hath no fury like a woman scorn' held as much meaning for me as it did at that moment..

"Motherfucker, you have GOT to PAY for this shit!" I said aloud, now inebriated.

I reached for the bleach bottle, unscrewed the cap, and proceeded to let it pour freely from the spout as I walked up the carpeted stairs into the bedroom. I doused the bed with bleach then continued walking in this manner throughout the house, till there was no more bleach left in the container. I entered the dining room and turned the glass china cabinet completely over, breaking all of the dishes inside, some of which were quite costly. Fuck it! The coffee table in the living room was my next target. With all the strength that I could muster, I lifted and returned it to the floor in a crashing thunder.

"Now, THAT felt good," I said talking to myself, "but I think that I can feel a little better!"

I entered his recording studio, gathered as many cd's and tapes as I could carry, walked upstairs, and placed them inside of the microwave.

"Let's see… what would be the cook setting for cd's and tapes? Oh yes" I said, continuing to ask and answer myself, "no doubt it would be high… for 'high' ya like me now!"

I laughed as I pushed the timer for thirty seconds and watched the contents fry. I retrieved another bottle of wine, then walked back downstairs into the laundry area to put in another load of clothes. I walked back into his studio and poured wine onto every piece of electronic equipment that I could, emptying the bottle. The last act of revenge was directed toward his other pride and joy, his jaguar. I found it amazing as to how easily a key could be broken off in the door lock, especially when struck at full force a few times with a hammer!

"Now motherfucker, I can leave you with some degree of satisfaction." I said aloud. I felt that what Parker has taken from me was far more than this material bullshit that can always be replaced. My heart can't.

Parker's plane was due to arrive at Atlanta International at 1:45pm, so it would probably be around 3p.m. or after before he reached home. I called Jerome to help me transport a few of my belongings to his parent's home. If it weren't for his help, taking time off from work today to help me move, I would've had to make several trips back and forth in my small PT Cruiser. I looked at my watch, trying to gauge the time. It was 2:27 p.m. We were moving at a good pace as we didn't have that much to move. Everything pretty much belonged to him. I had only one more suitcase full of clothing to carry to the car, but before doing so, I asked Jerome to give me a few minutes alone. He understood and waited for me outside in his car. I walked around feeling very emotional and sad, thinking that because of Parker's selfishness, my life has been uprooted. I walked into the living room, starring at the fireplace and thought of our first night together.

"What the HELL is going on here?" Parker yelled.

I'd been so deep in thought that I'd not heard the sound of the cab outside. He surprised the hell out of me! His eyes were as big around as doughnuts, and mine were too.

"There's been a robbery." I said in a calm, dead-panned voice.

As I passed the window inside, I saw that Jerome had gotten out of his car and was walking toward the house. I was relieved because neither Jerome nor I knew for sure what Parker's reaction would be. Parker walked further into the house, stepping over the detached leg of his coffee table.

"A robbery?" Parker repeated in disbelief. "Shit, are you alright baby?"

He motioned toward me to comfort me. I stepped back.

"As well as I can be under the circumstances." I said.

"Did you call the police?"

"No. There's nothing they can do. Unfortunately it's out of their jurisdiction."

"What the hell are you talking about Raven? Out of their jurisdiction?"

"It was my understanding that the Atlanta police doesn't have the authority to interfere in L.A. matters." I said, looking deep into his eyes for some sign that he's comprehending what I'm eluding to."

"You're not making any sense at all!" Parker said, now agitated with me and my logical 'nonsense'. "I want to know what has happened to my damn house, and damnit, I want to know RIGHT FUCKING NOW!" he demanded.

Jerome, now standing in the doorway of the house, walked toward Parker, as protector just in case he made a move toward me. Parker finally noticed the suitcase that was near me.

"Raven, no!", he said as almost a plea.

His eyes revealed that he now understood the situation.

"Please baby. I never meant to hurt you. I love you Raven! Don't leave me baby, please!" Parker begged, his eyes filled with tears, and of course mine were overflowing.

"Parker, you've made a choice, and now, so am I. For three days I've had to bear the burden of knowing what you did, with whom you did it, even how it was done. I have but one question... why? Why Parker? Was I not enough?"

"Raven, honey, if I could take back that night, I would..."

"You would... you would what Parker? Make certain that it was a stranger you were fucking so that I'd never know?"

""Baby, it's not like that." Parker interrupted. "Please let me explain."

"Explain? You CAN'T explain fucking my SISTER! There is no explanation for that! What can you say to me? Oops? It slipped?"

"Jerome", Parker said, "can you talk to her? Can you help me man?"

Jerome looked Parker squarely in the eye.

"Yeah man, I can talk to her..."

I looked at Rome in utter disbelief that he'd say that.

"...but no," he continued, "I CAN'T help you. You hurt my girl." Jerome looked toward me. "Come on Raven, let's get the hell out of here."

Jerome grabbed my suitcase. I walked with him to the door. Parker quickly walked toward me, grabbing my arm.

"Baby, I made a mistake and I'm..."

"I know the line Parker, 'I'm sorry', right?"

We both looked at one another in silence, realizing that 'we' had come to an end. Yes, unfortunately I still loved him, but I knew that I couldn't be with him anymore. I needed time away from him, time to forgive, but never would I forget.

"You know Parker, I loved you so much that there was nothing that I wouldn't have done for you; but what you've stolen from me, what you've robbed from my heart..."

"Baby, I'm sorry. Please forgive me."

"...my trust, my joy, my dignity" I said through my tears. "...YOU FUCKED MY SISTER! What you've done can never be recovered between us. 'We' are lost forever."

With that, I turned and walked out of Parker's world.

Chapter 10:

The club was packed. I gave the room a quick once over and noticed that there were very few people sitting alone; most everyone was coupled or in small groups. The sound of the band was penetrating. Jerome, Anita, Sheila, Mitch, Trent, Delores, and myself made our way over to what appeared to be the last available table. We were a couple of chairs short, so Mitch and Trent stood next to the table. Jerome said that he'd talked to Parker and told him that I was in town for the weekend, but that he, Parker, wouldn't be able to make it tonight. Seems he'd already made plans. Oh well. I must admit that I was disappointed that I wouldn't get to see him, as it has been nine years since we'd dated, but I tried not to let my disappointment show. I responded indifferently to his absence.

"Well, his loss", I said looking toward Sheila.

She agreed with me.

"There are so many fine men in here", as she turned her head from side to side. "I think that I'll go over to the bar and take up scouting position from another angle, she said grinning.

"I'll walk with you Sheila." Trent said. "I'm ready for a drink myself."

"Are you kidding?" Sheila snapped. "I don't want you walking with me Trent! Somebody may mistake you for being my date."

"And Lord knows, we don't want that, huh?" Delores said laughing, mocking Sheila.

"Damn Sheila, the man just wants to get a drink!" Mitch said.

"Well, I think that Trent is a big enough boy that he can get a drink without walking with me, now can't he Mr. Mitch." Sheila said sarcastically.

Mitch didn't respond. Jerome stared at Sheila in disbelief while shaking his head slowly from side to side.

"Look Trent," Sheila said directing her attention back to Trent, "count to twenty, then come over… but don't stand next to me either."

"All this for a drink? I don't believe this shit Sheila!"

We all laughed.

"Don't you understand anything Trent? You'll hurt my chances."

"Hell, judging by the way you're walking in those new shoes, it looks as though you're already hurtin' girlfriend." Delores said.

Everyone laughed again. Sheila had to chuckle at that one herself. It was really nice to be around my old friends again. I missed them so much.

"What do y'all know? Absolutely nothing!" Sheila said smiling, then stood up from the table, "Well, you know where I'll be."

Sheila walked over to the bar and stood right next to a tall, good-looking man. It was almost as if she had a honing device on; she'd found her first prey of the night. Just as Trent was instructed, he waited for a brief moment then walked over to the bar, remembering not to come within a fifteen-stool radius of Sheila. We laughed.

"Does that girl have any shame." Jerome said laughing.

"Look who's talking!" Anita said. "It hasn't been too many years ago that you wrote the book on picking up women!"

We all nodded our heads.

"I heard THAT!" Delores said in agreement. "I think Howard University's female population is still reeling from your reign of terror."

"Those were some good times, weren't they?" Jerome said, looking at Mitch.

Mitch nodded his head in agreement.

"They sure were man. They were the best of times. Damn good times, man!" Mitch said, his smile growing wider and wider, as though he were reliving those days.

"Really good…"

"Mitch!" Anita interrupted. "I believe we all HEARD you the first time! You sound like a broken record, for goodness sake." Anita said sharply.

"I was just agreeing with the man honey." Mitch said in his own defense.

"Then maybe you'd like to share with us your memories you're experiencing so that we can all smile like a cheshire cat too." Anita said, visibly jealous.

"Now there you go again, getting yourself all worked up over nothing. You see who I chose to be my wife the day after graduation now, don't you? You know there's no other woman for me but you baby." Mitch said, with Anita looking at him coldly.

Mitch bent down toward Anita and kissed her lightly on the lips. She responded in kind and gave him a smile.

"Let's dance." Mitch said.

"O.K." Anita agreed.

They floated onto the dance floor and were 'in love' again.

"Damn, what was that all about? I didn't know that homegirl had such a short fuse." I said.

"Yeah, and seems to be growing shorter and shorter every time we go out". Delores said.

"Does anyone know what's going on with them?" I asked.

"They're having serious money problems… an investment that went bad." Jerome said.

"Oh no! That's too bad." I said.

"Yeah, it is." Jerome replied. "I don't have all of the specifics, but it seems like Mitch was taken by a con man for about seventy thousand dollars, the bulk of their savings."

"Damn! No wonder homegirl's on edge." Delores said.

"Mitch is too. This is the first time in months that I've not seen him stressed out." Jerome said.

"Wow! That kind of money is nothing to sneeze at." Delores said.

"I KNOW that's right." I said.

"Well, I told him that when he feels he wants to talk about it, I'll be there for him." Jerome said.

"Good Rome." I said, pleased to hear of his support. "That's what true friends are for."

The band was very good, but they were a far cry from Saega. Jerome told me that Saega performs at a local jazz club called The Crescent Moon whenever they're not playing on the road. To be totally honest with myself, I would like to see him before I leave… I think. My love for him was so deep and our breakup so painful, I wonder from time to time what could have been.

"I've got to go to the little girls room to powder my nose. Come and go with me Raven." Delores said.

"Women always do that shit." Jerome said smiling. "What's up with this running to the john in twos. Are y'all following some secret law according to Noah, traveling two-by-two?"

"Shut up Rome." I said jokingly. "Men, you just wouldn't understand!"

"No, I really want to know", Jerome continued. "Why do you need Raven to go with you to powder YOUR nose?" he asked.

Delores and I were getting up from the table, smiling and ignoring Jerome's question.

"Just look at the size of that snout." Trent said approaching the table from the bar, catching the tail end of Jerome's question. "She's gonna need at least hers and Raven's two hands to help her powder that huge motherfucker if she wants to make it back to the table before the place closes!"

"Fuck you Trent." Delores said laughing.

"Would you? I've got on clean drawers tonight."

"Ugh! You're gross!" I said.

Delores and I slowly made our way across the floor. The ladies room was on the opposite side of the room, so we took our time and absorbed all of the gorgeous male 'sights'. Mitch and Anita had just finished dancing and were heading back to our table. The band was taking a fifteen minute intermission.

"Damn girl, our timing is fucked!" I said disappointedly.

"What do you mean?"

"Well now the ladies room is gonna be crowded."

"Oh, I didn't know you really had to go." Delores responded.

"I didn't at first; now the closer we get, the more I have to go!" I said.

We chuckled. Just as I'd predicted, we were like human sardines packed in our own juices. We took care of our respective needs in the ladies room.

"I feel thirsty." I said. "Let's get a drink from the bar while we're up. I hear a Fuzzy Navel calling my name. Want one?" I asked.

"Naw, I'll get something with you a little later, O.K?" Delores said.

"O.K. I'll be over shortly."

Delores went back to the table and I proceeded toward the bar. I ordered my drink and as I waited, I noticed a man's reflection staring at me in the mirror behind the bar. He was seated at a table positioned on a raised platform, but from his angle he had a clear, unobstructed view of me. I turned around to find him, but as I did, the house lights dimmed and my vision didn't make the adjustment from light to darkness quick enough. When it did, he had vanished.

"Where did he go?" I wondered.

I looked around in a complete circle and I couldn't find a trace of him anywhere.

"Damn, that's strange." I mumbled.

A new band had come on stage. The music was very sultry. I took a sip of my drink and began to walk back to the table, when I heard it... felt it... saw it! I felt just like the woman in the Bible that turned into a pillar of salt because she looked back at the city. My mouth was agape and my eyes were transfixed on the image approaching the stage in silhouette. He was playing the sax while walking into the spotlight.

"Parker!" I whispered.

I became so immersed in Parker's performance onstage that I was not aware that Jerome was standing next to me.

"Surprise babe!" he said smiling.

"Shocked would be a more appropriate word Rome." I said, still looking toward the stage, spellbound.

"You o.k? Should I lead you by the hand?" Jerome said jokingly.

"That may not be a bad idea. I do feel a little weak."

We walked back over to our table. Mitch and Anita had returned from dancing and obtained two chairs from another group's table who'd gone to the dance floor, so we were now all able to sit together.

"I just love when he hits those high notes." Anita said. "The man's still got it."

"I think you're right Anita." I whispered under my breath. "That's what I'm most afraid of."

Saega played for about thirty minutes, then there was a break. A dj played tunes while another band prepared to perform the next musical set. Parker made his way through the crowd, walking toward our table, evidently knowing in advance where we were seated. My heart was racing frantically. Parker Whitfield, the man I had once dreamed of marrying, having his babies, and raising a family, was now a stranger to me and my new life. Suddenly my mind was filled with questions: what would be his reaction to seeing me? What will my response be towards him? Out of the corner of my eye, I could see Anita and Delores staring at me. Delores, sensing my anxiety, squeezed my hand from under the table and leaned over to me.

"It'll be alright sweetheart." Delores said.

I smiled, unable to respond verbally to her sensitivity. My head was spinning with uncertainty.

"I never knew why you two broke up", she continued, "but time has a way of healing old wounds… if one wants them to."

I looked away from Delores to find Parker already at our table.

"That was a slammin' set Cozy." Mitch said. "You get better and better every time I hear you play."

"Thanks man." Parker said.

They hugged one another, as they, too, hadn't seen each other in years.

"Yeah man", Jerome interjected, "you blew the hell out of 'Be My Girl'".

They hugged as well.

"Good to see you man. It's been too long." Parker said sincerely.

He looked towards the women of the table.

"Hello ladies… Anita, Delores…"

"Hi Parker. You were wonderful." Anita said. "I closed my eyes and just let the music carry me away."

"Thank you sweetheart." Parker said.

"Hey Cozy. The set was really nice." Delores added smiling.

"Thanks, I appreciate that Delores."

Oh oh! Now my turn. I felt like I had an alien in my chest trying to jump out to freedom; my heart was pounding just that fast. Parker looked at me.

"Hi Raven." Parker said.

Up till now, I'd avoided eye-contact with him, looking at either my Fuzzy Navel, at Jerome, or the wall. But now, I had to face him without any distractions.

"Hi Parker." I said.

"You look beautiful. Time's been very good to you."

"Thanks." I said with a slight smile, but not giving him any more conversation than one or two-word answers. I couldn't. I was... nerve-wrecked. I suppose everyone at the table sensed the uneasiness between he and I, and interrupted our "bumpy" flow. I looked over my shoulder to see Sheila returning to the table with a man she'd obviously picked up from the bar.

"So Parker," Trent said, "I was in your neighborhood a few months ago and was told that you'd moved."

"Yeah man, about three years ago."

"Where are you now, baby?" Sheila said harmlessly flirtatious.

"Hey Sheila." Parker said, acknowledging her presence.

They hugged.

"I'm in a new development called the Bouknight Estates. It's really nice, with an in-ground pool, a sauna, and a tennis court."

"Damn man, sounds great." Mitch said.

"Well man, I'm not getting any younger..." Parker said, "...and if I'm gonna take steps, I want them all to be forward and upward."

He looked at me and our eyes connected momentarily.

There was no question that I still felt something for Parker, but I couldn't define it. I'd gone from loving him to hating him, and now I suppose I'm somewhere in the middle.

A new band was now onstage and the live music once again filled the club.

"Ahhhh shit! That's my song." Sheila said.

She grabbed her pickup's hand and pulled him toward the dance floor.

"Mitch..." Anita said in a whinny, baby's voice.

"I know baby, I know! Say no more." Mitch said, knowing the significance of the song to Anita and knowing that she wanted to dance.

Jerome, never at a loss of female company, whispered in the ear of a woman sitting at a nearby table. Soon they made their way onto the dance floor. Delores and Trent joined hands and also left the table, leaving Parker and me alone... for the first time in nine years. Our breakup was very emotional and devastating in many ways. For nearly one year I mourned the death of our relationship: I went out with guys and 'dogged' them horribly as I felt Parker had done me. Somehow, however, I still felt that I'd not gotten Parker out of my system... out of my mind, my heart.

"Would you care to dance Raven?" Parker asked.

I did, but I didn't, if you know what I mean. I did, because I enjoyed dancing very much and Parker knew that; but I didn't because I would be wrapped in his arms and I didn't think I'd feel comfortable enough being there, engulfed by him.

"No, no thanks." I replied.

"O.K." he said smiling. "You know Raven", he said with a more serious expression on his face, "I've thought about you so often that I can't begin to tell you, but I knew that I'd only cause you more pain if I contacted you, so I didn't."

"I really don't see the point of this discussion Parker. We ALL made our own decisions, and we ALL have to live with them." I said coldly, hearing the sound of pain in my voice.

He lowered his head momentarily, then quickly looked away towards the dance area. I felt that I still had some 'darts' to throw, although he was making the situation all too difficult for me by behaving so nicely. I picked up my drink and swallowed my last drop of Fuzzy Navel. He offered to buy me another, to which I refused, but he insisted. He got a waiter's attention and ordered a drink for me and one for himself.

"You really do look beautiful Raven. I'm glad to see that you're doing well."

"Thanks. You look pretty good yourself."

We smiled at one another, Parker visibly happy that I've finally said something nice to him that wasn't covered with 'ice'.

"Raven, I'm not trying to dredge up the past or anything, but I do hope that one day you can find it in your heart to forgive me."

I didn't respond, just looked at him.

"Time and time again I've paid the price for my irresponsibility to you and I know that I blew the best thing that ever happened to me." Parker said sincerely. "Again, I'm sorry and I never meant to hurt you."

I teared, but turned my head so that Parker couldn't see my face clearly. The band began playing another number and everyone remained on the floor. It was "Love Won't Let Me Wait", one of my favorite old songs. Parker asked me once again if I'd like to dance. This time, however, I accepted. I lifted my drink and took a huge gulp in a feeble attempt to settle my quivering body. Parker was still a very good dancer and ANY woman that danced with him invariably looked good by default… including me.

There was silence for a few minutes, as we were both absorbed in the music. I started to feel a bit more relaxed and once again accepted his invitation to dance the next slow song. I must admit that he did feel good, but I was so unsure as to where my feelings stood about him. After the second dance, Parker said that he had to go backstage to check on Saega and find out if they would be performing another set. He asked that I walk with him so that the band members could say hello. I agreed, as I did have a friendship with Rachel and would like to see her. As we neared one of four rooms off of the backstage hallway, we ran into Shanai, the female vocalist. We hugged one another and made small talk about her life now as a mother of a three-year old and my life now as a legal assistant.

"Rachel!" Shanai called as we entered the dressing room. "Someone's here to get your autograph."

We both smiled with anticipation of seeing the look of surprise on Rachel's face. Rachel walked out of another room and screamed with delight. We embraced as she jumped up and down. She was genuinely happy to see me, to say the least.

"Are you now back in the area?" Rachel asked.

"Only temporarily. I'm here on business for the weekend." I said. "I'll be leaving Monday morning."

"It's so good to see you. So much has happened to me." She said excitedly.

Rachel proceeded to tell me that she has her own single out now and that she'll pursue a solo career next year, with the blessings of Parker and the band.

"Let me get my Blackberry so that I can get your contact information." We should always stay in touch. Girl, you left so abruptly…"

She caught herself, realizing after the fact that Parker was still standing there.

"Oh, I'm sorry Cozy… how insensitive of me. I wasn't thinking." Rachel said very apologetically.

Parker assured her that everything was alright then excused himself from the room to gather the other members of the band. When he returned, Will, Ozzie, and Butch were with him. They each hugged me and gave me a kiss on the cheek.

"What brings you to town Raven?" Will asked.

"I had a taste for some good jazz and knew of only one group that could give it to me, so I hopped on the first plane out of D.C." I said jokingly.

We all laughed.

Parker began discussing the agenda for the remainder of the night while I quietly sat and observed, feeling a strong sense of deja vu. I looked around the room and saw Parker's saxophone standing in the corner and remembered the last time I saw it. Then, too, it was standing in the corner, but in the studio of our home. They made a decision on their next set and we, Parker and I, were about to leave the room. Just then, there was a knock on the door and a female voice called out for Parker.

"Cozy, Cozy darling. It's me, Bridgette."

Parker immediately looked at me as if he'd seen a ghost.

"I'm sorry Raven. Just an annoying groupie." Parker said.

"You don't owe me an explanation Parker. I'm just here to see the band members, remember?" I said.

"He's not here Bridgette. Go away." Shanai yelled back toward the closed door.

"Yes he is. I saw him come this way. I just wanted to thank him, that's all."

"Send him a postcard." Butch said. "He's busy."

All of the men laughed, with the exception of Parker. His face was very serious and flushed. She knocked again, and this time pounding.

"Come on Cozy, open up!" the voice said irritated.

He walked over to the door and opened it reluctantly.

"Loverboy!" Bridgette exclaimed.

She reached both of her arms around Parker's neck and clasped her fingers together. Parker grabbed her arms and pried them from around him.

"Bridgette, what do you want NOW?" Parker said sternly.

"You, if you've got the time." Bridgette responded.

She focused only on Parker, as if the band members and I weren't even in the room.

"Bridgette, I'm gonna tell you this for the last time…"

"I know, I know!" she said excitedly, as if she had the correct answer to a Jeopardy question. "You like 'it' from behind." She said laughing.

"Wrong answer." Will said aloud.

I walked to the door, moving past the 'couple'.

"Raven, wait. This isn't what you think." Parker said.

He reached out for my arm, but I moved it just in time, missing his grasp.

"This?" Bridgette said looking at Parker with an attitude. "What do you mean by 'THIS?' Are you referring to me as 'THIS'?"

"Shut up Bridgette! Can't you see the guy doesn't want to have nothing to do with you." Rachel said, now coming to Parker's defense.

"Hold it! Everybody!" I said.

"Who the HELL is this?" Bridgette said.

I ignored Miss Bridgette and directed my comment to Parker.

"Look, if I weren't here, this whole scene wouldn't be an issue, so I'm leaving to let you continue on with your new… life."

"Yeah, you do that hun." Bridgette said.

With that, Parker flung her completely around and off of him all together. I'd already begun walking down the hallway back toward the front part of the club. Parker approached me from behind and grabbed my arm.

"Raven, wait a minute! She's a groupie! She means nothing to me."

I turned around to look at him.

"Wow, for a while I was beginning to feel that maybe you had changed…"

"I have Raven." Parker interrupted. I am a different man than before."

"No Parker, you're still the same womanizing, self-centered man I left." I said

"That's not true. You're not being very fair…"

"Fair? I'm pretty sure that you had to have given Bridgette some indication that this type of behavior was alright. So now that I popped up unexpectedly, she's suddenly an embarrassment, a crazed groupie."

"Raven, let me prove myself to you again." Parker pleaded.

"All you've proven to me, Parker, is that the more things change, the more they remain the same."

I turned and briskly walked down the hallway, hearing Will say aloud, "I can't believe he's losing her again!"

Believe it!

Chapter 11:

I didn't feel up to answering questions from the group, so I didn't return to the table. Instead, I went to the farther side of the bar, away from our table, so that I couldn't be seen. How foolish I was to think that Parker had changed; that we could possibly have a friendship. I was so upset, I wanted to leave the club, but in doing so would reveal more than I wanted to admit. I couldn't let Parker affect me this way. I ordered a drink and sipped it slowly, closed my eyes, and tried not to think about anything. The music was very loud, almost deafening.

"I was hoping that you'd not left the club." I heard a voice say.

I assumed the voice was that of Parker.

"Leave me the fuck alone." I said without opening my eyes. "I don't want people like you in my life, so fuck off!"

"And what kind of people are you looking for?" the voice asked.

Suddenly it dawned on me that this was not the voice of Parker. I opened my eyes and turned to find the face of the man who'd starred at me earlier through the bar mirror. I laughed as I apologized for my language. He took the opportunity to ask if he could join me, but I told him that I just wanted to be alone for the moment.

"A beautiful woman such as yourself surely should not be sitting alone." he said.

"I don't mean to be rude, Mr...."

"Hunter's the name. Wayland Hunter."

He extended his hand to shake mine and I returned in kind.

"Look, Mr. Hunter..."

"Please, call me Wayland."

"Fine, Wayland, I'm sure that you're a nice man and all, but I'm really not in the mood for…"

At that moment, I saw beyond Wayland's shoulders, Parker approaching. I suddenly felt trapped. He'd evidently come looking for me and I was glad that he could see that I was now in the company of another man; not alone brooding. Maybe he'd go away and leave me alone. Maybe they'd both go away and leave me alone! Parker stopped short of the bar and just starred in my direction.

"Where the hell is Jerome when I need him!" I thought.

If I walked away from Wayland, Parker would seize the opportunity to approach me. On the other hand, if I stayed at the bar, I'd be forced into unwanted conversation with Wayland.

"You're not in the mood for what?" Wayland asked, prodding me to continue my train of thought.

I wanted to say that I wasn't in the mood for any more lines of bullshit, but considering my options and the fact that Parker was standing nearby, I chose to favor Wayland's agenda.

"I was just thinking that I wasn't in the mood for sitting anymore." I lied. "I'd like to dance, if you don't mind."

"Mind? This would be my pleasure." Wayland said with a smile that revealed a slight gap between his teeth.

He took my hand as we walked through the maze of tables and chairs toward the dance floor. Parker, seeing this, could only stare, as he was a man without a 'claim'. He turned and walked back toward the stage. Wayland was a man of about forty-ish with distinguished salt and pepper hair. He stood about six feet tall and was a bit overweight. It didn't detract, however, from his looks, as he was indeed a well-kept black man. He was dressed in a tan-colored suit with a very "noticeable" diamond ring on his pinky finger. Wayland attempted to make conversation with me, saying that he was a financial planner with offices in Atlanta, Baltimore and Chicago. He went on to say that he'd been a longtime accountant with the Internal Revenue Service and decided to embark on his own business, providing financial advice to "up and coming" blacks. I was half listening to him at this point, as his conversation was boring. I could think of nothing I'd like more at that time than to leave. I looked around the room for Jerome, but could not find him anywhere. As our bodies slowly moved and turned to the music, I looked over to our table to see some of the group seated there, but not Jerome. Just then Wayland turned around to look at a hand patting his shoulder.

"Do you mind?" Jerome said very courteously to Wayland as he cut in on our dancing.

Wayland looked at me and saw the huge grin on my face and knew right away that he had been dethroned. He moved aside to let Jerome ease in and, without missing a beat, Jerome clasped his hands in mine and continued the rhythm of the dance.

"Am I glad to see you!" I said.

"Yeah, I saw the look on your face and knew." Jerome said laughing." "I thought I'd bail my girl out."

"You, sir, are a true southern gentleman." I said in a terribly-imitated southern drawl.

There was a brief silence.

"Rome, I hate to be a nuisance, but…"

"You want to leave?" Jerome asked kindly.

I smiled with relief that my friend understood so much about me without me having to actually verbalize everything to him.

"Yeah, I'm feeling claustrophobic in here." I said.

The music ended and we walked toward our table. Out of the corner of my eye, I saw Wayland standing near the bar smiling as he sipped his drink and watched Jerome and I leave the floor. I turned my head and looked directly at him. I gave an apologetic smile. He raised his drink as if saluting me then turned around and faced the bar. I felt awful now. I knew that I'd used him as a smoke screen from Parker, but I could now see that HE also knew that he'd been used.

Jerome and I arrived at the table with everyone already assembled. Coincidently, they too were now bored with the club's atmosphere and discussed stopping by another. I, quite frankly, wasn't in the mood for club hopping and let everyone know that it was alright if they continued the evenings entertainment without me. Besides, Jerome had met a young woman that, I was sure, he wanted to get to know better. I said goodbye to everyone and they all left in their respective cars. Jerome and his new companion dropped me off at the condo, then they went to rendezvous with the others at some other club. I felt kind of relieved that I was alone…to think… to rest… to reflect. I relaxed in the comfort of Jerome's jacuzzi and thought of all that had transpired tonight. For the evening to have begun with such promise was disappointing to realize that it has now fizzled to no more than wishful thinking. Then I thought of Wayland. He was probably a man of fine qualities, but I didn't even give him a chance. Again, I've let Parker control the outcome of my life... of MY happiness. This was unacceptable. If I had it to do over again, Wayland would not have been my diversion but rather my refuge. If only I had it to do again.

Several hours later, the screaming ring of the telephone jarred me from my restful sleep. My natural instinct was to answer it, but after my eyes adjusted to its unfamiliar surroundings, I thought better about doing that. After all, this is a bachelor's home, and I didn't come down here to create any trouble for him with his 'women'. The third ring activated the answering machine.

"Hi baby." the female voice on the answering machine said seductively.

Jerome used to always leave the volume up on his machine to screen his calls. I smiled, thinking it's good to know that some things don't change.

"I waited up till 3. What happened to you?"

"Jerome, you have no shame", I said to myself smiling.

"You know all work and no play makes Jerome a dull boy", the voice continued, "and we can't have that... now can we? Give me a call when you can. Good-bye baby."

I turned over to resume my rest and noticed the clock.

"Shit, 10:30 a.m.!" I said with surprise.

I pulled myself out of bed, took a shower, and proceeded to the kitchen to prepare breakfast. I used Jerome's last three eggs in the refrigerator and fixed an incredibly delicious omelet, when I heard the door open.

"Lucy, I'm home!" Jerome yelled out in a bad 'Ricky Ricardo' voice.

"Is that you Ricky?" I asked, playing along.

Jerome walked into the kitchen to find me perched on the countertop eating.

"Mmm, that smells good! Any more?"

I motioned to the frying pan on the stove. Jerome helped himself to some leftover omelet.

"So, you managed to find your way back home I see." I said smiling.

"Yeah, it was an offer I couldn't refuse."

We laughed.

"So, what would you like to do this beautiful Saturday morning?"

"I don't know. I haven't had a chance to sought things out yet. I just got up about an hour ago." I said.

"Well, I know this may sound a little boring to you, but I wanna get you down here."

My arm froze from its motion of putting food into my mouth. I looked at Jerome with skepticism.

"What are you talking about, Rome?"

"There's a Job Fair happening at the Civic Arena today. It only costs five dollars for admission, but I think this would be a good start in getting you down here in Atlanta." Jerome said somewhat excited.

"Rome, I'm not sure about moving down here. My mind's not made up on that." I said with reservation.

"It's sponsored by the Chamber of Commerce," he continued, totally ignoring my statement.

"Rome!" I interrupted.

"You said that you weren't happy in D.C.: men that you don't care much about, a job that you admit is wasting your talents, plus I miss you and want you here with me." he said sincerely.

I smiled.

"Raven, sweetheart, the opportunities are limitless here. You don't have anything of any real significance tying you to D.C."

"Rome, you're sounding like a commercial. The Atlanta Chamber of Commerce needs more representatives like you." I said chuckling.

We finished breakfast and made our way into the living room.

"Ahhh!" I sighed, enjoying the view from the window. "You know things are never as bad as they seem after a good night's rest." I said, looking out over Atlanta's skyline.

Jerome walked over to the stereo and put on a Sade cd.

"Yeah, I heard that your backstage appearance had become a bit... crowded, shall I say?"

I turned to look at him, now sitting on the couch, smiling.

"And from who, might I ask, did you hear of this?"

"Oh, a sexy little song bird."

I thought for a second.

"Does this 'song bird' go by the name of Rachel?" I added smiling, deducing that Rachel and Shanai were the only other women backstage that knew me, and they both knew of me and Jerome's friendship.

"Could be." Jerome responded, not willing to divulge the name of his source.

I walked over to the couch and sat down next to him."

"You know Rome, as I relaxed in the Jacuzzi last night, I realized that I've not fully moved on to the next plateau, the next level. I think that I was still, in a way, open to the idea of Parker having some place in my life. Not necessarily my MAN, but perhaps a friend. Now, however, I see that I need to be completely rid of him so that I can progress. Does that make sense to you?"

"I absolutely understand what you're saying". Jerome responded.

He hugged me and sort of whispered in my ear.

"That's why it makes more sense than ever for you to attend this Job Fair. This would be a great first step towards your new plateau; don't you see that?"

For as long as I've known Jerome, he's always had very effective abilities of persuasion, and this was no exception. After all, he did have a point. What was I afraid of?

"O.K. knucklehead, you won. I'll go to the Fair."

"Great! I'll go with you. This'll be a good thing Raven. You won't regret it."

"I hope not Rome. Atlanta's not been very kind to me this trip. I'm losing faith." I said smiling.

"There's bound to be something for you here; never give up faith baby."

Jerome's advice to me that day would play back over and over in my head during the next few weeks: 'there's bound to be something for you here; never give up faith baby'… and he was right. There WAS something out there for me, something that anticipated my arrival.

Chapter 12:

The Civic Arena was crammed with all kinds of people: white collar workers blue collar workers, and even what appeared to be homeless people. I wore my navy blue suit that I wore down to Atlanta from Washington on Friday. My expectations of anything happening today was very low, but surprisingly enough, there were about six companies there that expressed an interest in me. Unfortunately I wasn't prepared to show them any substantiation to my claims of vast experience. They wanted a hard copy resume and I didn't have that. They did, however, ask that I send it to them upon my return to Washington. I told them that I was looking for a company that I could grow with; become a part of. They all seemed to love that bullshit. Whatever works!

After nearly three hours, Jerome and I left the Arena and visited his parents. They lived in close proximity to the Arena and, if only for a brief visit, I couldn't very well come to Atlanta without seeing them. When we drove up, they were relaxing on the front porch, rocking in their chairs. They looked just like a Norman Rockwell painting. I smiled with joy in seeing them, and they reciprocated.

"Well, if it isn't my baby!" Mrs. Cunningham exclaimed.

She rose from her chair to greet us, walking down the driveway. I ran toward her and gave her a big hug and kiss.

"I remember the days when you used to call me your baby." Jerome said, pretending to be jealous.

"Oh hush up stinker!" she said jokingly, hitting him playfully on his butt as he passed by.

"Hi Mama C." I said.

"Hi baby. Let me look at you."

She stepped backwards, holding my hands to either side of her and looked me over.

"You're still as beautiful as the first time I saw you!"

"Thanks Ma. That's very kind of you to say."

We walked toward the house, my arm wrapped around her shoulder. Jerome had already taken up position on the porch to hug his dad, who was now standing.

"Hi Poppy." I said.

"How's my girl doing?" he said as he hugged me.

"Fine. You guys been O.K?"

"Oh yeah. Things couldn't be better Raven."

Mr. Cunningham looked over at Jerome.

"Boy, go inside and get a chair for Raven."

"Oh no Poppy!" I said. "I'll just sit right here on this step."

"Nonsense." Mrs. Cunningham added. "Jerome…"

"Ok, ok! I'm beginning to feel like a stepchild around here."

We all laughed. Jerome returned with two chairs for he and I. We were having a good time just talking and catching up on our lives when Jerome's cell phone rang. He looked puzzled at his phone, not recognizing the number, then went inside the house to take the call. When he returned, he said that it was Rachel wanting to catch up with me before I leave Atlanta. She told Jerome that she'd left a message on my cell, but when I didn't respond, she assumed that I'd be with him. He gave me his phone to call her back. I excused myself and went inside to talk to her.

"Hey girl! How are you doing today?" Rachel asked.

"Pretty good". I responded.

I explained to her that Jerome and I had gone to the Job Fair and that my phone was in my purse turned off.

"What's up?" I continued.

"I know that you're leaving Monday morning, and I just didn't want you to leave with our last time seeing each other to be surrounded by such chaos."

"Forget it Rachel. I have. Besides, you didn't have anything to do with that situation." I said. "You're still my bud." I said, reassuring her of our continued friendship.

"Good." she said with relief in her voice. "Look, I'm having a few friends over…"

"I can't come if he…"

"Don't be silly Raven. I wouldn't dream of doing something like that to you, especially with what you went through last night." Rachel said.

"Thanks Rachel."

"So, you'll come?"

"Sure, I'll stop through." I said.

"And ask Jerome if he'd like to come too. You know he's always welcomed at my house." Rachel said in a seductive voice.

We laughed. Years ago, Jerome and Rachel had a brief affair. Between his busy work schedule and her hectic touring with the band, the relationship collapsed.

"O.K., I'll ask him. What time?"

"My place, around 8:30 p.m. It'll be just a few friends, very informal, and hopefully very relaxing. A little food, a little fun, and dress comfortably."

"Sounds good. See you there."

I returned outside and relayed the message, but Jerome said that he couldn't make it. He'd made plans with the woman he met from the club last night. Evidently she's saying or doing something right to keep his attention. Good for her. Well, I have no problems in 'going it alone'; sometimes I prefer it. He was sweet enough to let me use his car, as his date was picking him up. I suppose modern times call for a modernized woman. You go girl!

Not including myself, there were a total of about ten people there. Rachel seemed very happy that I came and introduced me to everyone. Besides her, I'd not known anyone. She had everything set up so nicely. We all converged in the backyard under a screened canopy. The table was set beautifully and party lights surrounded the outer perimeters of the yard. Jazz filtered from inside the house as we talked and sipped our drinks, waiting for dinner to be served. I was having a great evening; just the way I'd like to be leaving Atlanta… relaxed.

"Ding Dong."

"Could someone get the door?" Rachel shouted from the kitchen window. "My hands are a mess.'

"I'll get it." I responded.

I walked through the kitchen, into the dining room, past the living room, and down a narrow hallway leading to the front door.

"Ding Dong", the bell rang again.

"Who is it?" I asked.

I got no response Again I asked, and still again no reply. I looked into the peep hole to find no one there. I went back into the living room to look out of the window to get a better view as to what was on the other side of the door. I saw a man running toward a black Mercedes. He retrieved an attaché from the passenger seat, then turned to make his way back to the house. I opened the door.

"Well, well, well. If it isn't my damsel in distress." he said smiling, but visibly surprised.

It was the guy from last night. Wayland.

"Oh, hello". I said, just as surprised.

Rachel entered the room and hugged him.

"Wayland.   Good to see you."   she said.   "Raven, this is Wayland…"

"We've met". I interrupted, smiling.

"Really? I didn't know that you two knew each other." Rachel said confused.

"Well, we do and we don't." Wayland said as we walked down the hallway toward the backyard.

He sat his case on the floor in the living room beside the couch.

"I met Mr. Hunter…"

"Please," Wayland interrupted, "I insist that you call me Wayland."

"O.K. I met Wayland last night at the club."

"And how do you two come to know one another?" Wayland asked, pointing to both Rachel and myself.

"Raven and I go waaay back." She knew me during the early days of Saega, and we also have mutual friends."

"Use that term loosely." I said smiling, eluding to Parker.

I was unsure as to the connection between Rachel and Wayland, but didn't feel comfortable enough to ask… at least at that time. By no means, however did I want to give any impression that I was interested in Wayland. Men are truly the last thing on my mind for right now.

Some guests had left the backyard and went to the family room where a movie was already in progress. Rachel, Wayland, and I sat in the backyard and talked. It was here that I learned that Wayland is Rachel's financial planner and investment advisor. I suppose that because she is now embarking on a solo career, she will need guidance on what to do with her new-found wealth that is sure to come. I was so impressed with her; the rare combination of talent, brains, and beauty. There's no stopping that energy. I also learned that Wayland was 43 years old, widowed, and the CEO of KIF Unlimited Investment Firm.

"So Wayland, what does 'KIF' stand for, if anything?" I asked.

"KIF is the acronym for Keeping It in the Family."

"Oh no!" Rachel exclaimed. "You're gonna get him started. He doesn't go anywhere without talking shop to someone!" she continued, holding her hands in a jesting fashion to either side of her face smiling.

"Let me go and check on the food. It should all be ready by now."

She hurried away.

"Back to your question Raven," Wayland continued. "KIF refers to keeping money in the Afrocentric family of investors. We should make a concerted effort to seek, invest, then reinvest in those businesses owned and operated by Blacks. That is the only way we'll all reach financial success." Wayland said with conviction.

"Oh, I see. Well you make a good point."

"I want to make more than just a good point, my dear. I want to make a difference. Do you think that Johnson Publishing Company or Black Entertainment Television got to where they are by themselves? Hardly. They had to have investors to believe in their vision and contribute their support as well as capital. Consequently, if the company's successful, you will rise as well."

Wayland spoke of his business with a niagara of passion. He said that he started the business fifteen years ago with his wife, with a mere three thousand dollars, and within six months they had reached a ninety thousand dollar profit! He says that he looks at himself as a middleman of sorts, matching potential growth capital with a potential growth company. Wayland said that he filled a need for financial advisement and guidance within the Black community, thus KIF. Business had been doing so well lately that Wayland says that he's now in the final stages of expanding his downtown Atlanta office to include another location on the east side of town. I was very impressed by this 'thinking' man. I could use one of those in my life right now.

After dinner, we all played charades in teams. It was crazy fun. Everyone was laughing and enjoying. I hadn't done anything like this in many years, and it felt wonderful! After the game, we all chit-chatted, then called it a night.

"Can I give you a lift Raven?" Wayland asked politely.

"No thanks. I drove also."

"Then surely a nightcap somewhere. I could follow you." he continued, not wanting the evening to end.

I asked myself, "what could it hurt; a nightcap with a friend of a friend." That's harmless enough, isn't it? Well, isn't it?

Chapter 13:

"After last night in the club, I didn't expect to ever see you again."
Wayland said, as we sat across from one another at a local bar near
Jerome's house. "I'm glad that I was wrong."

"I am too." I said smiling back at him. "After leaving the club, I
regretted not having spoken more to you. It was just an awful night
for me." I said.

"I understand. We all have those days."

"I suppose so." I said, exhaling a long sigh.

Wayland was a talker! He talked about his firm, KIF, and it's many
investments in and around Atlanta, including his 2.1 million dollar
investment in the Sarafian. I was impressed. He talked about his wife's
passing and how he submerged himself into his work.

"Before I realized it, ten years had passed. Although I was very
successful, I was also very lonely." Wayland said.

"You don't have someone special in your life to balance things out?"
I asked him.

"Listen who's talking". I thought. Where is my balance? Living
a life of 'dates'; relationships that begin with promise and fizzle out
within a week; a sea of men, most of which I don't even remember their
names.

"No, not really." Wayland said, now looking out of a window to
the street. "I've just not found 'her' again."

"Your wife?" I asked. "You're looking for your wife to be reincarnated
in another woman?"

"I don't know. Maybe I am. She was such a good woman; the best thing to ever happen to me." he said, almost tearing.

"I bet she was quite a lady," I said, trying to give him some solace, "but Wayland, how do you expect to go forward with your life if you're always looking backward? Always grieving?"

He looked at me and a calm expression blanketed his face. He smiled. I smiled too. It was a nice moment and I felt good that I may have helped him think about rebuilding a bridge to his life. Maybe. Well, I'd like to think that I did.

Wayland seemed to have an unquenched interest in me, asking about my work, my family, my friends, and my love life, starting with Parker. He was particularly interested in my current relationship with him. I explained that Parker was just a man that I used to date, not going into much detail. After all, it, nor I, was any of his business. I told Wayland that the relationship had ended long ago and that Parker and I are no longer in contact. I told him how dissatisfied I am with my present job and that I've been thinking of moving to Atlanta.

"Well that's great." Wayland said. "Atlanta is THE place for opportunity, especially for Blacks."

I laughed, thinking of Jerome and his lecture earlier today about his hometown.

"You're beginning to sound like a friend of mine, who's always raving about Atlanta and it's 'streets paved with gold'".

"Dreams can come true, Raven."

He asked for my telephone number. I gave him my business card which had my office number only. He responded in kind with his card.

"Have a pleasant trip back to Washington, Raven. I'll be in touch real soon." he said smiling.

"I had a good time talking with you Wayland."

While driving back to Jerome's house, I felt I'd just met a very significant person in my life... a friend that I hope would be a life-long one. Maybe even someone that could become a little closer than that, who knows. Surely not I.

My plane was not due to depart Atlanta until 9:15a.m., so I had plenty of time to get to the airport. I awoke around 6 a.m. Jerome wasn't able to take me to the airport because of a presentation he had to make at work. No problem. He did, however, leave me a note on my nightstand:

> Good morning sleepy head. It was great having
> you here for the weekend. Wish that you had more
> time available. I'll try to call you before the end of
> next week to chat. Please seriously consider the
> BIG MOVE. This is where you belong… closer to me,
> and closer to your 'piece of the pie'! I took the liberty
> of arranging for a cab to be downstairs at 7:30a.m. to take
> you to the airport. Miss you already.
>
> Jerome

What a guy! Too bad he doesn't have a brother, cousin, friend… someone just like him, for me.

"Good afternoon Ms. McNair. How are you today?"

"Good afternoon Alvin. I'm a bit tired, but fine, just fine." I said, having just left Baltimore/Washington International Airport. Alvin pushed the button to close the elevator doors and, as habit would dictate, pushed the button for the thirteenth floor.

"Are you going out of town today, Ms. McNair?" Alvin asked.

"No, I'm just returning from a weekend business trip to Atlanta." I said smiling.

"Hope everything went O.K." he said nicely.

"I think the 'boys' upstairs will be pleased." I said.

We both laughed.

During our climb, he stopped on a few floors to load and unload passengers, greeting everyone with his warm smile. It was amazing seeing him operate in the morning. For those who actually worked in the building, you would only have to tell him once the floor on which you worked. After that, he remembered without error. Alvin had been an elevator operator since, I think, God created the seventh day! Seriously, it seems like he had been working here forever, and had always been pleasant, even to the snobs that got on with him and looked down their phony noses at him. Alvin was the first kind face I met when I started working for the firm. I'll never forget that.

"Here we are, Ms. McNair." Alvin said.

The doors opened and I got out of the elevator.

"You have a good day now."

"Thank you Alvin. You have the same."

Hearing the elevator doors closed reminded me of the thud of prison bars slamming. I had a sinking feeling in my stomach, and was very much aware of the anxiety, the unhappiness, the feeling of impending doom, every time I reported to work. I walked down the hallway and opened the ceiling-high glass doors of Hainesworth, Fascell, and Younger. There was a maze of cubicles and along the walls were private offices and conference rooms. Toward the end of the room were the partners' offices. I walked toward my cubicle to put my bag down, as it had become quite heavy. I followed the cubicle configuration to my desk. No sooner had I set my bag on the floor did my intercom ring.

"Good afternoon Raven."

"Treyci." I said, not pleased that she'd been watching me through the glass and had not given me time to get settled.

"Mr. Fascell would like to see you right away, and bring the paperwork with you." She said in her 'all business' voice.

"I will be there as soon as I come back from the ladies room. I do have time for that, don't I? Or does Mr. Fascell wish to do some mopping up in his office?" I said sarcastically.

She didn't say anything in response.

"I thought so." I said. "I'll be there in five minutes."

I took my finger off of the intercom button and turned to walk away from my desk.

"Make it three." Treyci said.

I looked toward her glassed office and could see the smirk on her face, satisfied that she got the last word in on the matter. After returning from the ladies room, I hurried toward Mr. Fascell's office. Treyci announced me to Mr. Fascell, then instructed me to enter.

"Raven, please come in."

"Thank you Mr. Fascell." I said.

He was seated at his desk flipping through some papers. To his right stood one of the other partners, Mr. Hainesworth, looking out of the window. Seated on the couch were three associates, also reading and scanning documents.

"I'll take that off of your hands now, my dear." Mr. Fascell said, motioning toward the signed brief I'd obtained from Atlanta.

He looked it over then passed it around the room for the other's to inspect.

"Great! This is all we need to solidify our position in the case." Mr. Hainesworth said. "Good work honey. That'll be all."

I stood there in disbelief for a few seconds. "Good work honey?" I thought. What a jerk Mr. Hainesworth was! And then to dismiss me without so much as a 'thank you'. That did it! A snicker erupted from one of the associates, as though this shit was funny. I was so enraged, I felt that I had to say something to this chauvinist asshole.

"Mr. Hainesworth, I'm sure that you are aware that honey is a substance produced by bees..."

All of the associates' mouths dropped open with shock at my bold display. I was sort of shocked at myself too, and I knew that I was treading on thin ice, but for the first time since I've been an employee for the firm, I really didn't care if this meant the end of the road for me. I just didn't care enough anymore.

"...I'm also sure that you are aware that it is scientifically impossible for me to be mistaken as the bi-product of insects."

Mr. Fascell began laughing hysterically, which infuriated Mr. Hainesworth even more.

"Therefore, I'd appreciate it if you'd refrain from making such comparisons, as the two are as dissimilar as an intellectual..."

I turned to look at Mr. Fascell.

"... and an imbecile."

I then looked at Mr. Hainesworth.

Quickly, I marched out of the office. As I passed Treyci, I informed her that I'll be leaving early today because I've developed a splitting headache. I hated my job, and having to work for chauvinist people like Hainesworth made it that much more difficult. I walked to my desk, thinking about what Jerome said about Atlanta's job opportunities. I opened my file drawer, took out a copy of my resume, and proceeded to rework it.

"Ring, ring, ring".

"Shit!"   I mumbled to myself, dreading having to answer my phone.

"Ring, ring, ring".

"Ms. McNair speaking. May I help you?" I said.

"You certainly may."   the voice responded. "I've been thinking about you lady."

"Wayland?"

"Yes. I have a business proposition for you that I'd like to discuss with you, when you have a moment."

"I must admit, your timing is impeccable. I was just thinking of my options."

"Having that kind of day, huh?" Wayland asked.

"I sure am, and I don't know how much more of this I can take." I said.

"Sounds to me like you need a change, like ASAP."

"I think that you may be right."

"Well, I think I've got what you need."   Wayland said almost seductively.

I smiled, and could feel that he was smiling too. .

"Oh you do, do you?"

"Well, of course you'll have to be the judge of that, but I would like to talk to you about it."

I gave Wayland my home telephone number.

"Call me tonight around nine, O.K?" I asked.

"Sure thing. I'll talk to you then."

"I'll be waiting."

I gathered my belongings and walked toward the elevator, waiting again for my friend Alvin to appear.

"On your way out to lunch, Ms. McNair?"

The doors of the elevator slammed shut.

"No Alvin." I said very reflectively. "Let's just say that I WAS at lunch; now I'm on my way out."

Chapter 14:

Just as I'd imagined, Wayland was the consummate businessman, calling exactly as promised. His offer was for the position of Finance Coordinator for KIF's newest location in Atlanta. I told him that I was flattered and appreciated his help, but that I didn't feel qualified to accept. I had no experience in finance whatsoever! He insisted that prior experience was not a requirement and that he could show me all that I needed to know, sort of an on-the-job training position. Wayland went on to say that the job paid ninety three thousand dollars for my first year, and afterwards I would receive an additional ten percent bonus on the initial investment capitol supplied by any new clients that I signed up with the company. I immediately thought of all of my friends and maybe even friends of theirs that I could sign. That would surely bring me well over a six-figure salary.

"Wayland, it all sounds too good to be true. I don't know what to say."

"Say yes!" Wayland urged.

"I don't know." I said smiling. "Why me?"

"Don't sell yourself so short, Raven." he preached. "Look, I want you. I look at you and see great potential in KIF's future."

My mind raced frantically, thinking of all sorts of questions. Where would I live? How soon would he need me there? Who would be responsible for my moving expenses? I articulated these questions to Wayland.

"Slow down a minute." he said laughing. "You don't need to worry about a thing. I have, or should I say that KIF Unlimited owns an apartment building nearby the new office site. You could stay in one of the apartments for a few months until you find a place of your own." Wayland said, trying to calm me. "In terms of moving expenses, KIF is prepared to pay eighty percent of your costs."

I couldn't believe what I was hearing.

"This is too enticing Wayland. There must be a catch."

"No catch at all. I'm just a man who makes a living at finding, developing and making deals, and I have a good feeling about this. You are the person that I want to fill this position." he said decisively.

There was a brief pause of silence.

"Well?" Wayland prodded.

"Well, I wouldn't be able to come down for another four weeks or so." I said, allowing myself a short vacation between jobs.

"If that's the earliest time that I can get you, so be it." he said, unphased by my delay. "It doesn't officially open until the fall, so it'll still leave plenty of time for training and honing your new skills."

Again, there was silence.

"Wayland, let me sleep on it till Wednesday, alright?

"Sure Raven, but don't think too long." he advised. "We wouldn't want to let opportunity pass you by, now, would we?" he threatened.

"I'll talk to you on Wednesday." I said. "And Wayland, thanks."

"My pleasure, my dear."

I hung up the phone and screamed with excitement. This was definitely not my kind of luck. Could this be happening? Is this my chance at a slice of the proverbial pie?

Over the next few days, I didn't get much sleep, excited not only with Wayland's lucrative offer, but also with the response I received from six Atlanta firms that I'd sent my resume. Isn't life peculiar that way? either nothing's happening or everything's happening. I called Jerome and Darlene to get their opinions about my prospects. As one would imagine, they were all very happy for me; that I'm finally in the position to pick and choose. I also called Rachel, since she was a friend of Wayland's to hear if she had anything further to add about him.

"Damn, I knew the man liked you, but I think you've made him loose his mind!"

We laughed.

'Well, there's nothing on earth better than a man with no mind and plenty of money!" I said.

We both laughed again.

"So tell me, how did you first meet Wayland?" I asked.

"A good friend of mine at the time was a background singer on the circuit for years. Well, she wrote a book about the behind the scenes of the music business call "Just A Fly On The Wall."

"I remember that title. Parker had a copy of that book in the library of our home." I said.

"It wouldn't surprise me. Her book generated a lot of buzz and brisk sales. It was very clear that she was gonna make a lot of money."

"So this is how you met Wayland?"

"Yeah. Her agent arranged a meeting with her and Wayland to discuss investments and financial options, and she asked me to accompany her to the meeting. When we left him that day, I held onto his business card, figuring that I'd need it myself one day."

"Smart move Rachel."

"Yeah, I called him a few years later when I signed on with my new record company for my solo career."

"Ok, so he's on the up and up?" I asked, trusting her opinion of him.

"Let me put it to you this way Raven; with Wayland Hunter in your corner, you can't go wrong. I say go for it!"

As I'd promised, Wednesday had arrived, and a decision was due Wayland. I accepted his offer.

"KIF Unlimited Investment Firm, Diane speaking." I heard my secretary say into the telephone. "Mr. Cunningham? Sure, just a second sir while I check to see if Ms. McNair is in."

She put the telephone line on hold and buzzed me.

"Ms. McNair, you have a call on line three. Mr. Cunningham from Rubenstein and Craft."

"Thanks Diane." I said. "I'll take it."

"Well, well, well! Now who's too busy for whom?" Jerome said.

"I know, I know, but…"

"You've been down here for a month now and I've only seen you once! What's the deal?" Jerome continued, not acknowledging my attempt at an explanation.

It was true. I didn't anticipate the grueling thirteen-hour days, but Wayland assured me that this would not be the case after my training period.

"Jerome, I told you that I'd be working some long hours." I said.

"Well you can't keep this pace up for very long." Jerome warned. "Sooner or later, something has to give."

"Actually, things should level off in a few more weeks."

"Good." he said relieved. "Have you gotten settled into your new apartment yet?"

"Almost. I've been trying to make time for all that I need to do, but between working these long hours, unpacking, and shopping for household goods, it really doesn't leave me much excess time." I said.

"Well, let me know if I can be of any help babe. You know that's what family's for."

Our conversation ended abruptly because of an important meeting that I had to attend with Wayland that almost slipped my mind. We concluded our conversation with a promise to try and see each other before the end of the week. What would I do without my good friend, my 'brother', keeping me sane. I hope that I'll never have to find out. Today I was to be introduced to the other KIF employees at the main office in about an hour. My office consisted of only five people: my secretary Diane, two investment agents, Marcus and Gevan, and Joy, a data entry specialist. The main office, on the other hand, was much larger, consisting of about twenty people. There were three people who answered directly to Wayland. They were the Financial Directors. Each Director had three investment agents working under them. For every three agents, there was a data entry specialist who inputted their information into the KIF server. Then, of course, Wayland and each Director had their own secretaries. Wayland had engineered a well-organized machine, and I was proud to be a part of his empire.

Traffic was horrific, and as a result, I arrived about ten minutes late for my meeting. Wayland was none to pleased, to say the least. He verbally insulted me in front of several employees and made some remark about me taking my paycheck and investing in a watch that could keep the correct time. I was speechless! How dare he! Was he just having a bad day, or was this the true monster behind the mask? My first impression with my new colleagues will be that of admonishment by 'DAD'! After a lack-lustered introduction to the staff, Wayland asked that I come into his office.

"Look Raven, I have a very strict policy of punctuality here at KIF. This meeting was called for 1:30 p.m. exactly, not 1:30 a.m., not 1:45 p.m.... 1:30 p.m.!

"I understand that Wayland," I said in my defense, "but I got held up in traffic."

I didn't dare say that I almost forgot about it altogether.

"No excuses! Then you need to leave your office earlier."

I was appalled and actually kind of afraid of him. He looked as though he could've killed me... for being ten minutes late?!?!

"So, I was to be made an example of?" I asked.

"No, you were not the example. At least half of all of my employees have made the same mistake too, but only once. Today you had your turn, and just don't let it happen again." he said. "Do we understand one another?"

"I think that we do. You know, you were so nice to me that I almost forgot that you are my boss. This, unfortunately, was a hard reminder of that fact. You are my boss, not necessarily my friend. I understand" I said coldly.

I turned to walk out of his office.

"Is there anything else, Mr. Hunter?"

"I think that you're being much too sensitive, Raven." Wayland said. "This will be a valuable lesson that will one day serve you well, and you will thank me for it."

"What an asshole." I thought.

"Being late can mean the difference in securing a contract and losing one, in obtaining a profit on a trade or losing thousands... millions!"

I looked him directly in the eyes.

I understand Mr. Hunter." I said in a defeated tone. "Can I go now?"

"Yes, you can go."

The days that followed were filled with intense training. It was almost as if he turned up the fire on me. He crammed so much information into my head that I thought at times that I'd crack. But the more I felt that way, the more I was determined to prove that I can handle it. I don't even know who I was trying to impress more, Wayland or myself. I absorbed all that he taught and was eager to learn more and more. I sat in on his negotiations with clients and witnessed deals and investments ranging from hundreds to thousands to millions of dollars. I learned how to apply the most appropriate statistical formulas for use in solving any given circumstance, and I met some very powerful and influential people along the way. Throughout my training, however, I often questioned myself, asking 'why me'? Why did he choose me? I finally heard a voice answer back saying 'why not'? After that day, I never questioned myself about it again.

Chapter 15:

Four and a half months had passed since being in Atlanta and, needless to say, KIF Unlimited had become my center. It seemed that I spent more time at work than anywhere else. Although Shanai and Delores would stop by the office occasionally to have lunch with me, I still felt very lonely and isolated from the rest of the world. I'd not seen my friends in a long time and I missed them greatly. Long hours were spent studying material that Wayland tested me on constantly. Occasionally I'll help a client with a routine tax issue, but basically most of my time was spent learning everything KIF related. Wayland keeps telling me to just be ready when the time comes, and that time is fast approaching.

One evening, while working a typical late night at my office, I got an unexpected visit from Wayland. He'd been out of the country for the last several weeks taking care of some investment accounts in Switzerland, and the last that I heard from talking to his secretary, Gwen, was that he was still there. I suppose being the President of the firm gives you the luxury to jet set all over the world with little or no notice. Must be nice. Wayland traveled quite extensively, taking an overseas trip at least every month or so. Without any warning, Wayland barged into my office.

"I knew it!" Wayland said, smiling with delight that his prediction was correct. "I thought you'd still be here working."

Startled, I looked up from my desk. I was sure that I'd locked the street-level doors to KIF, as I was the only one there at that time of night.

"Mr. Hunter!" I said startled.

Seeing the terror on my face and realizing that he'd almost caused me a coronary, he apologized for his sudden intrusion.

"What can I help you with, sir?" I asked smiling politely, though still frazzled.

"Raven", Wayland said, walking further into my office toward me, "don't you think it's about time you dropped the 'Mr. Hunter' formality?"

I rose from my desk feeling very uncomfortable. I walked toward the file cabinet to do 'busy' work.

"Isn't 'Hunter' your name, sir?" I said with my back towards him.

"Listen Raven, if I didn't do it before, I apologize."

I knew immediately that he was referring to the so-called introduction he gave me to the staff. And yes, I did still harbor ill feelings towards him because of it.

"What are you apologizing for Mr. Hunter?" I asked, pretending not to know.

"I didn't take you for one that plays games Raven." Wayland said.

I didn't respond. He leaned forward on my desk, no longer smiling. I looked up at him.

"Friends?" Wayland asked smiling as he extended his hand as a gesture of a truce.

I placed my finger to my temple as though I was considering his offer, but in actuality I, too, wanted us to be friends again.

"Sure." I replied, shaking his hand.

"Good. Let's celebrate by going to dinner."

"I smell an ulterior motive cooking!" I said jokingly.

Wayland smiled.

"I'm famished. I would think that you must be as well."

"Well, to be honest, I could use a bite." I said.

"Great, then that's settled."

We went to a small restaurant within walking distance. It felt great to finally get out, even if it was with my boss.

"You know Raven, I've received some encouraging feedback from some of my clients about you." Wayland said, as we were being seated in the nearly empty restaurant.

"Is that so?" I said smiling.

"Yes it is. Mr. Dorsey said that you handled his problem with the IRS and the business tax credit like you'd been doing it for years."

"It was nothing." I said modestly, but very proud of my achievement.

"Oh, but it was young lady. It was! Mr. Dorsey has been a long standing client of KIF and has never given ANY associate of KIF a compliment. He's a very tough man to please, but somehow you broke through the ice."

"I'm just glad that I was able to adequately represent the firm." I said.

"Well, I just wanted you to know that your hard work and dedication to KIF hasn't gone unnoticed."

"Why thank you Wayland." I said proudly.

"Yes, things are shaping up rather beautifully." he said as he looked into my eyes smiling.

I returned the smile.

We ordered, ate, and returned to KIF. I decided to say goodnight at the door, as I was finished working for the night. I was glad that Wayland persuaded me to go out to dinner. The breather did me good but the weather had become very windy. A storm had been forecast for our area. As I proceeded to cross the street toward my car, a clap of lightning ripped through the sky. Out of my peripheral vision I saw that Wayland was not walking away, simply standing there watching me. I turned completely around, stopping in the middle of the street.

"Is there a problem Wayland?" I asked.

"You could say that." he said, with a strange look on his face.

I walked back toward him, puzzled.

"I was given a ride over here by an agent in my office, so now I'm afraid that I don't have access to my own transportation." he said, somewhat embarrassed.

"So… is there something you'd like to ask me?" I asked smiling, deliberately trying to make his situation more difficult

"Ms. McNair," he said making a jestful bow, "could I please trouble you for a ride to my quaint abode?"

I laughed aloud. The charming, witty gentleman I'd met at Rachel's party had returned. I liked him this way…a lot.

"I think that I might be able to accommodate your request." I said smiling.

When I got to Wayland's house, it was approaching midnight, however the distance and the time seemed to no longer matter when I laid eyes on his 'quaint abode', as he called it.. It was truly nothing short of a palatial mansion. At the entrance to his eight-acre estate, there were two stone pillars to either side and a small sign embedded within them that read: HUNTER HEAVEN, NO TRESPASSING BEYOND THIS POINT. He reached into his wallet and took out a small electronic device and aimed it toward an iron gate. It slowly opened, permitting us to get a little closer to 'heaven'. Still holding the device, Wayland pushed another button as he pointed it to open the garage doors. Of what I could make out in the dimness of the light, he had three classic cars parked near the back wall of the garage, and a red Ferrari that glimmered in the night. My eyes were as big as saucers. I had no idea that he lived this grand. 'Wow' was all that I could muster to say. I was indeed speechless. Wayland thanked me for the ride home and invited me inside for a nightcap, but I refused. He urged me not to leave because of the lateness of the hour, and because of the heavy rain, but I insisted that I must. Had I gone inside, it would not have taken much coaxing to convince me not to make the return trip back, considering that I was already very tired. Besides, how would that look: the employee spending the night with her boss! Well actually, no one would have to know, but the last thing I wanted was for things to get out of hand. Maybe another time, another place.

Business was going extremely well for KIF, achieving a record-breaking quarter for new clients. Wayland had begun a recruitment campaign a few months ago to attract more middle-income clients and first-time investors. The campaign was a huge success and it was now paying off big dividends. Wayland offered the agent who generated the highest influx of new clients an all-expenses paid trip for two to Jamaica. The agents' competition was fierce, and as a result, KIF prospered. Wayland found it necessary to send four additional agents to me from the main office because of all the recent activity.

During my last conversation with Jerome, he told me that Mitch and Anita were still struggling desperately and needed a financial boost.

He had already loaned them some money to get a few creditors off of their backs, but they needed substantial remedies. I figured that I could give them that, through a small investment with KIF. I knew that there were at least four investments that Mitch and Anita may be able to afford. I recommended to Mitch that they go with the Energy Tax shelter which involved solar heat duct panels. The investment was guaranteed to triple over the next five years, when it reaches it's maturity. The minimum investment amount was five-thousand dollars, and, as Wayland explained, the risk of such an investment was nil. The benefit of the return would be felt almost immediately by the investor because they would then quality for a tax exempt status on their federal and state income taxes. I thought that this would be the perfect vehicle for them. As a result, Mitch withdrew five-thousand dollars from his baby's educational fund. The money had been as a gift from Anita's parents, and Mitch was adamant about Anita not finding out that the money had been withdrawn. I assured him that the money, upon it's maturity date, could be replaced without Anita being the wiser. I then thought of other friends and family that I could help. Out of roughly twenty calls, I did manage to convince others: Jerome's parents, my brother Elliott, my cousin Calvin, my girlfriend Sheila, my Uncle Adam, and Mr. Alvin, the elevator operator from Washington, D.C. For those that could not be in Atlanta to represent themselves, I sent them a Power of Attorney form that they signed and returned to KIF, giving Wayland authority to act on their behalf in this investment matter.

As the Financial Coordinator, I was responsible for scheduling group orientations with all new clients and assigning an agent that specialized in that area to explain and address questions about the particular venture. For every investment avenue that KIF offered, there were two expert agents that dealt solely with that tax shelter. I then collected the money, processed each investor into the KIF system, and submitted a purchase order form to Wayland for that investor. The purchase order detailed the equipment involved in the shelter, and also specified how many units were being bought for what price. It was a lot of work, but I was satisfied to finally be doing something concrete instead of studying! I assigned Darren as the agent to familiarize a group of 186 people about KIF's Solar Heat Duct Panels energy shelter. At the conclusion of one orientation, another would commence two hours later to address a different group of investors. Everyone was very excited and eager to put their money to work for them, legally and within the system. I must admit, the money collected was staggering. After arranging and supervising three different groups of investors that first day, over a million and a half dollars passed through my hands! Nine hundred thousand of which was generated from the very popular Solar Heat Duct Panels energy shelter alone! All of the studying that I've endured over the past few months: KIF rules and regulations, problem-solving formulas, document preparation, IRS requirements and restrictions; was in preparation for this day; a day that questioned whether or not you had what it takes to succeed in the business. Thanks to Wayland, I have found my answer.

Through the day, Wayland could look out of his penthouse office down onto the floor of KIF at the bustling activity. He could monitor the amount as well as the number of transactions that were taking place via his computer. Unquestionably Wayland was a very happy man, as we all were. The campaign was a success and we were helping people begin to achieve financial independence. Wayland was often concerned with clients experiencing problems with an outside accountant who was unfamiliar with these shelters, so he took on the task of providing KIF clients with income tax preparation as well. I considered Wayland to be a financial genius, and I wanted to learn everything I could from him. Finally, with the help of Wayland Hunter, I WILL attain my piece of the pie... ala mode.

Chapter 16:

The only word that comes to mind when I think of Jamaica is enchanting. The magnificent greenish-blue of the water, combined with the clear, blue sky, the unrelenting sun and the beige hue of the sand all made for a wonderful Caribbean experience. It was as if looking at a giant-sized postcard; it took my breath away.

After the six-week run of KIF's New Investors Recruitment Campaign, Wayland decided to not only provide a trip for Eli, the top agent, but also to the entire twenty-five member staff! He did, however, give him a generous bonus of twenty-five hundred dollars to honor the original terms of the campaign. Wayland decided that everyone had worked so hard that even his expectations of a successful campaign were surpassed. I'd often wondered how Wayland managed to keep his employees loyal and happy and at the same time pushing them to their limits. He expected everyone to give him, or should I say KIF, their all. It isn't hard to understand how he's achieving this. I mean, c'mon, the entire staff to Jamaica? Who's going to object to this kind of treatment? Exactly my point… no one!

Once settled in my room, I went outside to the hotel's pool area. Gwen, Wayland's secretary, was seated at a table with a couple of women that I'd not met before. They were laughing and drinking and just soaking up the sun. Everyone seemed so relaxed and happy. I walked over to join the group. Gwen introduced me to her two girlfriends, Sandra and Elizabeth, who were also the only two women agents under KIF's employ. Coincidentally Elizabeth, like myself, was also an alumnus of Howard University, attending just a few years before I did.

We bonded immediately. Sandra, on the other hand, was a little more reserved. She was considerably older than we were, probably in her mid to late fifties. I perceived her as a no-nonsense woman with not much personality and even less points for her looks.

There were a variety of evening activities that the Hotel sponsored, including a late night luau. I looked forward to attending that, but in the meantime, Elizabeth and I wanted to go into town and shop at the Bazaar. The Bazaar is where the Islanders can make money from the tourist for their wares. Anything from arts and crafts to clothing to furniture can be obtained for a very reasonable price. Sometimes the vendors would arrange special 'deals' for you, depending upon your pocketbook. It was an interesting experience. It reminded me of a used car lot, and you were making your first car purchase. Luckily enough for me, Elizabeth had been to Jamaica several times before and knew the ropes. We eventually returned to the hotel carrying sixteen bags between us. Sixteen bags! As we made our way through the lobby, we noticed a group forming for the Dunn's River Falls excursion. Elizabeth explained to me that this was one of the Island's highlights. She said that not only was it a beautiful sight, but adventurous too, because you actually climb rocks to the top of the fall. Wow! That sounded exciting to me and I wanted to participate.

"Don't leave without me Earle." I yelled toward him as Elizabeth and I walked toward the elevator. "Let me drop my bags off in my room and I'll join you all in a few minutes." I said.

"O.K. Raven." Earle replied.

"Are you going to go Elizabeth?" I asked.

"No, I think I'm gonna skip it this time." Elizabeth said. "I've been there four times before. It'll be lots of fun."

"What'll you do in the meantime?" I asked my new friend.

"Believe me Raven, there's plenty to do in the Caribbean… plenty." She said smiling a very broad smile.

"You sound as though you already have something planned." I said trying to pry.

The elevator arrived and Elizabeth and I boarded.

"The tour guide'll be here in about ten minutes." Earle shouted toward me before the door closed. "I'll sign your name on the list."

"Great. I won't be long." I said, as the elevator door closed.

I pushed the button for the ninth floor. KIF booked the entire floor of the hotel for it's employees. Elizabeth lowered a few of her bags onto the floor and pushed the elevator for the fifth floor. I was puzzled.

"Well?" I said, pursuing my previous line of questioning now that we had the privacy of the elevator.

"Well what?" Elizabeth said laughing.

"Fifth floor?" I asked. "What's on the fifth floor?"

Elizabeth smiled.

"You don't want to know," she said still smiling, "but I'll tell you one thing, I've never met anyone like Wayne before."

"Wayne?"

"A friend from my previous trips."

"Gotcha." I said, finally understanding.

The elevator arrived at the fifth floor. She picked up her bags and got off.

"You have a wonderful time at the Falls, and I'll probably see you tonight sometime."

"O.K." I said. "You have a wonderful time too."

"Not to worry." She said smiling as the door began to close. "I have a wonderful time just THINKING about him." Elizabeth said, and with that she turned and walked very briskly down the hall, never looking back. I smiled, thinking of what awaited her.

"I used to get excited that way… long ago." I thought. God, it's been so long since I've felt that way about a man. I missed that.

When the door opened on the ninth floor, Wayland was standing there with a group of people that I'd recognized as employees from the main office.

"Hi there." Wayland said jubilantly.

"Hi Wayland. Hello everyone." I responded.

They all replied with a similar greeting. I walked out of the elevator and into the crowd.

"You seem to be going the wrong way." One man said.

"The story of my life." I joked back.

They began boarding the elevator.

"Raven, aren't you going on the Falls trip?" another man asked.

"Yes, yes I am, but I first have to drop off my shopping bags to my room."

"Well, you'd better hurry." Another man interjected.

The crowd was crammed into the opened elevator as the doors began to close involuntarily.

"All aboard!" another man yelled out, as if a conductor on a train.

Everyone was on except for Wayland.

"Stanley," Wayland said, "you all go on down and I'll help Raven with her bags. We'll meet you in the lobby."

"Sure thing boss." He said as the doors closed.

Wayland grabbed five of my seven bags from my hands. We walked down the long corridor hurriedly.

"This is really nice of you Wayland. Thanks."

"No problem at all." Wayland responded. "I tried ringing your room earlier to find out if you were going on the trip or not, but there was no answer. Now I see why."

He raised his arms shaking the bags.

"You were making an investment into the Jamaican economy!"

We laughed. We dropped off the bags and joined the others just as they were beginning to board the shuttle that was to take us to the yacht. From there we would sail to the Falls.

Elizabeth was absolutely right. It was great fun. Everyone had to lock arms and climb UP THE WATERFALL! I was terrified at first, but quickly adapted. When we reached the top, we all applauded, hugged, and screamed with wild excitement. We conquered the mighty Dunn's River Falls! On the return trip to the hotel on the yacht, the official partying began. I didn't want to get too relaxed and reveal more of myself than I needed to with the group, so I conservatively stayed with mild drinks that I knew I could handle. There were nearly eight small groups of people talking and enjoying themselves. I was mingling with them all, weaving in and out of varied conversations. Richard, one of three Directors of KIF, who apparently began his festivities a little earlier than the rest of us, approached me from behind, putting his arms around my waist. My eyes grew slightly with surprise.

"Can I get you another drink sweet thang?" he said softly in my ear.

"What you can do is get off of me Richard, that's what you can do!" I said sternly.

I pried his hands off of me.

"Oh I see that you're not a team player?" Richard said scornfully.

A couple of people from the group tried coming to my assistance, sensing a potential 'scene' and realizing that Richard was inebriated.

"C'mon Richard. Knock it off." Darren said.

"Yeah Richard," Gevan chimed in, "give the young lady a little room to breathe."

"Who asked you anything tough guy?" Richard replied antagonistically. "Since when did you become her bodyguard?"

He returned his stare back toward me and continued his harassment.

"So, I understand that Wayland mail-ordered you in all the way from Washington, D.C." he said very cunningly. "Must be something real sweet and special about you, huh?"

"You're a jerk, Richard." Gladys said, giving him a challenging stare.

She walked away from the group shaking her head from side to side.

"So I suppose Wayland has already staked his claim on you." Richard continued.

Humiliated, I turned to look at him squarely in the eyes.

"You're a disgusting son-of-a-bitch Richard." I said, then threw my drink in his face.

I excused myself from the group and walked to the farther side of the yacht. I leaned over the railing and watched the waves hit against the side.

"I feel that this was partly my fault." A male voice said to me.

I turned around to see who was willing to share responsibility for someone else's stupidity.

"Gevan." I said surprised.

I smiled. Gevan was one of two agents assigned to my office. He was a very gentle man, unlike the other agents who seemed more suited for this kind of work: aggressive, tough-skinned, and sometimes downright ruthless. Because of Gevan's mild manner and honesty to his clients, he was also the least productive agent that KIF had. He always says that it was more important to him to 'put the people first and not their pocketbooks'. But again I stress that he's in LAST place.

"You can't possibly feel you were to blame for an obnoxious drunk." I continued.

"Well, I saw him coming your way, eyeing you ever since you came over by the group. I should've made a move to pull you away or something," Gevan said sincerely, "then none of this would've happened."

"Nonsense. If it didn't happen here, it would've happened someplace else. The alcohol just gave him the courage to approach me. And I think that it was better to have it here than in maybe a more secluded place."

"I guess you're right about that." Gevan said.

"He thinks he can get away with anything just because he's Wayland's brother-in-law."

"What?" I said shocked, not believing what I heard.

"Yeah." Gevan continued. "I don't understand why Wayland still keeps him around. Everyone knows that all he wants to do is drink and carouse. Richard's secretary, Tamera, is really the one who's keeping his group of agent's productive, and Wayland knows it too."

"Well, why do you think Wayland keeps Richard around?"

"I don't know", Gevan said thoughtfully. "Maybe out of some sort of family loyalty. Afterall, Richard was married to Wayland's sister. I don't know... maybe, maybe not."

"Do you know something Gevan?" I whispered, smiling devilishly.

Gevan smiled too. We both broke out into laughter.

"Let me freshen your drink." Gevan said, dismissing any further conversation about Richard.

He took the glass from my hand and walked over toward the bar.

"I wonder what he meant... maybe, maybe not?" I said to myself. "What the hell is going on inside KIF and what does Gevan know?"

The Caribbean music filled the air at the luau. It took place on the beach, near the water's edge. There were score's of beach lanterns spiked into the sand on tall poles. Some people waded in the water, while others played games, and still others just drank, talked, and enjoyed the music. Four hours had passed and by now the effects of the partying were very apparent. The romantic setting of Jamaica combined with the alcohol gave way to office shenanigans to which I refused to be a part. People were pairing up and wading into the warmth of the ocean, some walked along the shoreline, and still others sought the sanctuary of their hotel rooms. Gwen, Tamara, Victoria, and myself declined several offers from some of our overzealous colleagues. Two or three others who could still differentiate honor to their spouses from their lustfulness also excused themselves. I began to feel like being alone, so I told Gwen and the girls that I'd see them in the morning, as we were scheduled for a buffet breakfast and a tour of a neighboring village. When I entered the lobby of the hotel, the desk clerk called me over.

"Ms McNair?"

"Yes." I responded.

"There's a message for you."

"For me? Are you sure?"

"Yes Maam."

He handed me the note. It read:

'Thought you might like to relax and unwind.
I set sail at midnight from Freedman's Dock.
Hope you can make it.'

The message was signed 'W.H.' I'd wondered what had happened to Wayland. I just assumed that he, too, was taking advantage of the 'liberal spirits' of his employees. I should've known better to think that Wayland would be a participant to such. I was glad that he wasn't there. I looked at my watch to see that the time was 11:40 p.m., so there was still time to meet him if I chose to do so. I was actually excited and flattered by his invitation. I had hoped to spend some time with Wayland during our time in Jamaica and was somewhat disappointed that I hadn't … at least up til now.

"Excuse me", I said to the desk clerk, "but can you tell me how to get to Freedman's Dock?"

He instructed one of the bellmen to show me the way. It was well within walking distance, located on the rear-side of the hotel, but the desk clerk didn't want me to walk it alone. As we neared the dock, I could see Wayland leaning over the railing of the yacht. The closer I got, the louder I could hear music playing. I recognized the artist immediately; Maxwell's Black Summer's Night cd never sounded more romantic than it did that night, under the beauty of the Caribbean sky. I thanked the bellman for escorting me and gave him a generous tip.

"Thank you beautiful lady." he said smiling.

I continued the walk alone, smiling with every step. When I was close enough to see the detail of Wayland's face, I could see that he was smiling too.

"Glad to see that you made it, mate." Wayland said. "I was just about to set sail."

"And leave me all alone? Wayland, how could you?" I asked jokingly.

Wayland met me as I ascended the gangplank, extending his hand to assist me. Soon, with Wayland at the helm, we slowly moved further and further away from shore. It felt very relaxing, even though I didn't have a clue as to where we were going. It really didn't matter though, because I trusted Wayland and felt very safe with him. We talked and laughed and enjoyed one another's company. Wayland was a wonderful conversationalist as he revealed more of himself to me than ever before. I felt a strong connection with him tonight. After nearly twenty minutes of navigating, Wayland dropped anchor at another dock. There were about nine other vessels there. He invited me downstairs to the galley, where he had a beautiful seafood dinner displayed on the table, complete with candles and a flowered centerpiece.

"Oh Wayland", I said surprised, "this is lovely."

"Not as lovely as you look tonight." he replied.

I blushed.

"I'm glad that you came back to the hotel when you did." Wayland continued, "because this meal would've been impossible for me to handle all by myself." he said smiling.

I returned the smile. After dinner we returned to the deck and relaxed on cushioned reclining chairs, marveling at the beauty that surrounded us.

"You know, I've been thinking of this moment with you for quite some time now Raven." Wayland said.

"What moment is that Wayland? Having dinner?"

Wayland smiled.

"Not exactly... but you're close."

We both laughed, understanding the tease.

"No," he said in a more serious tone, "I meant spending some quality time with you, that's all."

I smiled, pleased with the idea of his feelings being the same as mine.

"I like that." I said seriously.

Wayland looked deeply into my eyes and I in his. The atmosphere seemed so magical… so perfect for romance.

"You're so beautiful Raven."

He reached out his hand and took mine in his. Under the illumination of a full Jamaican moon, Wayland led me toward the master bedroom. Only the sound of the waves gently crashing against the yacht could be heard, only the warmth of his body could be felt, and only the desire in his eyes could be seen. Wayland's lips connected with mine and sent a sensation throughout my body that made me tremble. Neither of us uttered a word; we didn't have to. We knew what we wanted and where things were headed. What was there to say, after all? When the door to the bedroom opened, Wayland turned on a switch on the wall. I assumed it to be a light switch but the room remained fairly dark, with the exception of moonlight seeping in through the portholes.

"Maybe there was a blown bulb or a short circuit that caused the light not to work," I thought, "but hell," I continued my thought, "I don't need it anyway. I know where to find everything that I'll need!"

Wayland turned to look at me and starred for a long time. He lifted his right hand and felt my face, letting it slowly drift down my cheek and around to my neck. He brought his lips closer to mine, kissing me lightly and sensuously. I closed my eyes in total relaxation and enjoyed the moment. My body began to ache for him… for long-awaited passion.

"Raven, tell me that this is what you want." Wayland said. "Tell me that you want me."

I paused, not knowing how to respond. Did he mean 'did I want him' as in to fuck or did he mean 'did I want him' as in to be mine beyond tonight? I suppose the answer would be yes on both counts.

"Yes Wayland, I want you… I want you."

Now he could take that to mean whatever he liked. I could feel him becoming more excited, more eager as we stood against one another.

His kisses were now hard and passionate. He slid his hands up my dress. We both moaned when his hands came to rest on my buttocks, stroking and massaging my cheeks rhythmically. With his lips still touching mine, he guided me to the bed. I laid back and could see, through one of the portholes, a spectacular view of the water as it crashed against the dock. Wayland laid down on top of me and proceeded to caress and kiss and explore… and me to him. With my clothes removed, Wayland smiled with delight.

"Oh yeah, baby. I knew that you would look this way!"

"And what way is that?" I replied smiling, knowing full well that he was referring to my full breasts and curvaceous hips.

"So… so edible." he said.

"I can't believe that you could still be hungry, especially after eating such a magnificent meal." I said teasing.

"Mmmm", Wayland moaned. "With this kind of nourishment…"

He leaned forward and burrowed his head into my chest.

"…I can never be filled."

Unlike my past lovers, we didn't make love all night long, but I was far from disappointed. Wayland didn't have the stamina of the others, but what he did have was that added degree of experience. It confirmed the old adage that it does get better with age. Before drifting off to sleep, I remember looking toward the ceiling, smiling and satisfied, and thinking of how happy I was at that moment. The room seemed to be lit up with moonlight and with something else that I hadn't noticed before. On the wall, on the other side of the room, was a blinking red light.

"What is that?" I thought.

Wayland had already fallen asleep, so it was out of the question to get an answer from him.

"Probably just a security system." I rationalized.

I nestled closer to Wayland and once again smiled.

"It's nice to have security for a change."

Chapter 17:

As with all good things, at some point they must come to an end, and the Jamaican trip was no exception; a welcomed, yet temporary, departure from the rigors of the daily grind. The incoming mail at my office had piled up incredibly high for such a short period of time. It comprised the usual monthly office bills, a package from my sister, and the remaining pieces of mail were from people who wanted to take advantage of the special investment program that we offered during the recruitment campaign. I will have to forward their information to Wayland because he will ultimately determine whether to extend the expired investment to them or refer them to another program. Whatever he decides, I'm sure that he'll make some accommodation for them into some KIF investment or another. After all, it's still money, isn't it?

Nearly a week before the office trip to Jamaica, I spoke with Darlene over the telephone. She said that she had a surprise to send to me, so, of course the contents of this package held my surprise. I was very excited to know what it contained, as Darlene gave me absolutely no clues. I savagely tore open the manila envelope to reveal several newspaper articles from back home, and a note attached which read:

'…and to think it started as a dare! Call me soon.'
Love,
Darlene

The articles were from various dates spanning several months. My mouth widened as I read the headlines: 'Last-Minute Candidate Throws Name Into Ring'; 'Mayoral Field Widens To Three… And Growing'; 'Challenger McNair Just McMight!'; 'Incumbent Whitaker Digs Heels In For Tough Fight.'

I screamed aloud with joy. My secretary, Diane, ran into my office alarmed.

"Are you alright Ms. McNair?" she asked concerned.

"Yes, yes Diane." I said smiling. "I'm sorry for that outburst, but I've just received word that my sister is running for Mayor of our hometown!"

"That's wonderful!" Diane said, now also smiling.

"It sure is." I said.

I told Diane to hold all of my telephone calls so that I can, without interruption, do as my sister instructed. When I reached her on the telephone, we screamed with joy in each other's ear. I was so proud of her and even more proud to be her sister. She said that it began as a prank that snowballed.

"Before I knew it," Darlene explained, "people began taking me seriously, so I had to re-evaluate my position, and finally I became serious as well."

She went on to say that the family has been very supportive, and that Aunt Samantha and cousin Peter even work in the campaign office mailing out letters and pamphlets. Darlene had to step down from her position at the Newspaper because of her political run, but said the money that Mom and Dad left from the insurance is being used to make ends meet.

"I'm sorry that I can't be there to share this time with you," I said, "but I hope to be there real soon."

"I understand sweetie." Darlene said. "And when you do, I'll be right here waiting."

I hung up the phone after our conversation mumbling over and over to myself as if I were in a trance.

"My sister the Mayor… my sister the Mayor!"

Just as things were settling back down to a normal pace from the recruitment campaign, another tidal wave of customers hit our offices. It was now tax season, and as is KIF's policy, tax preparation to KIF investors is mandatory, and is written in very small print at the bottom of the investor's contract with KIF. All agents, with the exception of Paul's group of agents, will do nothing for the next several months but prepare income tax forms. There were literally hundreds of clients, so needless to say, the operation was once again very hectic. Wayland requested my two agents, Marcus and Gevan, to work out of the headquarters for the next couple of months as tax preparers as well. My job during this period was to continue processing the paperwork for the energy investment so that it could be included on their tax returns as a tax-exempt write-off. Wayland asked that I also work out of the main office, but only until the paperwork was completed. Compared to what the others had to do, I considered my job effortless, and projected that if I worked 12-hour days, I could be finished within a few weeks. The first day of working there went very smoothly, however the second day was one that I'll never forget. It actually set the stage of things to come. If only I knew then what I know now, but as it is with hindsight, it's always twenty-twenty.

Wayland, and a client I later learned to be Mr. Joseph Higgenbotham, were arguing in his glass-enclosed office. The blinds had not been drawn and therefore everyone on KIF's lower floor could look up and unobtrusively see what was taking place. An elderly Black gentleman in his 60's and a long-standing client of the firm, Mr. Higgenbotham stood eye to eye with Wayland, pointing his finger in his face in a threatening manner and swearing quite a bit. Wayland seemed to have had very little to say in his defense, although from time to time he'd try to calm Mr. Higgenbotham.

"Don't patronize me damnit! Mr. Higgenbotham yelled in a muffled, glass-filtered voice, "This is my life you're fucking with Wayland."

"Now Joseph, you should know better than this." Wayland replied.

"I should know better?"

Mr. Higgenbotham unexpectedly moved away from Wayland and sat down, resting his head in his hands. Suddenly he began to sob. Although from what I've seen so far was very confusing, the expression of anguish on Mr. Higgenbotham's face was undeniable. Finally realizing that he did not have adequate privacy, Wayland walked over to the window and drew the blinds closed, but by then it was too late. Everyone had already witnessed it.

"Alright, alright… everyone back to work." Paul commanded from the main floor. "the show's over."

"The show?" I questioned to myself. "What show were we tuned to?"

People began to disperse and hesitantly returned to their work, still able to hear the raised voices from Wayland's office. Still curious and concerned, I walked over to Elizabeth's desk to get her views on things.

"Mr. Higgenbotham has been the eleventh person THIS WEEK who's had a confrontation with Wayland." Elizabeth said.

"What is the problem? Is something happening with their accounts?"

"I don't know." Elizabeth said. "All I do know is what I've heard through the rumor mill, and that is that about sixty-three people, so far, have been contacted by the Internal Revenue Service."

"The IRS?" I said. "Those assholes! They make careers out of intimidating people."

"I know what you mean." Elizabeth agreed. "It has always fascinated me as to how widespread people's fear of the IRS extends."

"I think that people have more fear of the IRS than being shot at point-blank range." I said.

"Well for some," she replied, "the two are synonymous."

We laughed.

"I heard that the problem has something to do with some kind of code violation, but I don't know how serious it is or not." Elizabeth said.

I looked up towards Wayland's office.

"Well, there are at least two who thinks it's serious enough" I said, "Mr. Higgenbotham and the IRS."

"Wayland'll get the situation straightened out." Elizabeth said confidently. "I've seen him do it before."

"So this happens often?" I asked surprised.

"I wouldn't say often, but it does happen with more regularity around tax season."

"Well, I hope that he and Wayland can straighten things out for Mr. Higgenbotham's sake. He seems like such a nice old guy."

"He is, and has some pretty nice sons too." Elizabeth said.

I smiled.

"Now how do you know all of this, Miss Columbo?" I said jokingly.

"I know this because I happened to be here in the office a few years ago the day that two of his three sons accompanied him on their way to taking their Dad to lunch."

"Really?" I said with interest.

"Yeah. Muscular, attractive, and very single as I recall."

"Bingo!" I said smiling. "Just the way I like 'em."

"Me too girl. Good looking men like that don't stay single for long."

"Yeah, you're right." I agreed. "What do they do for a living?"

"One was a plumber and the other an electrician, and both ran their own successful businesses."

"What about son number three? You said there were three sons?"

"Aw, he's a loser." Elizabeth answered swiftly. "He's the bad seed of the family; always in trouble with the law and always relying on his family, particularly his father, to bail him out."

"Oh well," I said, "two out of three ain't bad."

Thirty minutes had passed and finally the yelling had subsided in Wayland's office. That was a good sign, 'cause I really didn't want to see the little guy end up with a heart attack or something.

"Well sweetie, let me get back to work." Elizabeth said.

She pushed an intercom button located near her telephone.

"Corey, could you come here please. I have about four dozen more completed returns for you to pick up."

"Be right over Liz." the voice responded.

"I'm not gonna hold you up any further." I said.

I got up from the chair to walk back to my temporary work station.

"I'll talk to you later, O.K?"

"O.K. Raven, and don't let this bother you too much. I'm sure that KIF will take care of whatever the misunderstanding is with the IRS."

We smiled at one another. As I walked away, I looked up at Wayland's office again.

"Don't worry Mr. Higgenbotham," I said to myself, "Wayland will take care of everything... He'll make everything all right."

That night, Wayland came over to my apartment and together we enjoyed a lovely meal and less than wonderful lovemaking. I attributed his lack of performance to stress. As we laid in bed, and exchanged small talk, I told him of Darlene's mayoral aspirations and of the newspaper articles she'd sent. He seemed happy for her.   I wanted to ease my way into a discussion about Mr. Higgenbotham and the other clients, but wasn't sure how to make the transition smoothly without getting a backlash.

"Hey baby," I said trying to gently broach the subject without getting Wayland upset any further, "I couldn't help but notice earlier today the conversation you were having with Mr...."

"Stay out of it Raven." Wayland snapped back. "Don't you have enough work of your own to keep you busy?"

"Well, I didn't mean any harm, baby. I thought that maybe I could be of some help..."

Wayland sat up in the bed, visibly irate.

"I see that you are losing your hearing in addition to your mind. Would you like to try for your job?" Wayland said in a very degrading and humiliating tone.

"What?" I said. "Lose my job for asking you a question? Just fifteen minutes ago, we were the only two that existed in the ENTIRE FUCKING UNIVERSE," I continued, "and now your ass is threatening me?"

I didn't know what to say to him... what COULD I say to him. I stared at him in utter shock for a few seconds. I couldn't distinguish who it was that I was talking to: Wayland my lover or Mr. Hunter my boss. I gambled and chose the former.

"You fuckin' asshole!" I blurted out. "You power-hungry, egotistical, control freak!"

I tore back the covers of the bed, grabbed my robe, and teary-eyed stormed into the bathroom. I slammed the door behind me.

"Raven." Wayland called out to me.

Of course I didn't respond. Afterall, what more is there to say. I turned on the faucets and patted some cold water on my face as I cried. I vowed to myself that from that moment on, things were going to be different... AGAIN! Yes, another of my many turning points.

"Honey", Wayland yelled, "I'm sorry. I admit that I overreacted. Come on back to bed." he demanded.

I continued to run the water, giving him no response.

"Look, there are some aspects of KIF that I don't discuss with no one, including you. That's just the way it is." he said.

I opened the bathroom door and returned to bed.

"Look, Raven..."

"Drop it Wayland." I interrupted, "there's nothing more to talk about."

"That's good, because it's none of your..."

"Hey," I snapped back at him, "I got your point! I will stay out of your business from now on."

"I just want you to totally understand what I'm saying." Wayland said as he nestled back down into bed, insensitive to his hurting remarks.

"Don't worry Wayland," I said to myself, "If I didn't understand before, I sure as hell do now... loud and clear!"

Chapter 18:

Although it was only for an hour, it was wonderful to see Jerome after not having done so in several weeks. I think we rejuvenate one another when we're face to face, and after last night's war with Wayland, I needed jsome rejuvination, badly! I shared with Jerome Wayland's peculiar behavior last night.

"Why didn't you put that asshole out of your apartment girl?" Jerome asked.

"I would've loved to Rome, but remember where I am..."

Jerome's head tilted to one side, obviously not understanding what I was trying to say.

"HE OWNS THE PLACE!" I yelled.

"Oh yeah." Jerome mumbled. "I forgot."

"Hey", Jerome said, his eyes lighting up, "you should probably give Sheila a call. She's a part-time real estate agent and could steer you to affordable properties."

"Good idea Rome." I said. "I'll call her tonight when I get home."

That night I called Sheila and told her that I was interested in her services: to find me a townhouse. I told her the amenities and price range that I felt most comfortable with. She assured me that despite my short work history with KIF, that it would be no problem qualifying because of my income and savings.

"I heard from Mitch that you were with the investment company KIF."

"Yeah, I'm with them." I said. "I ran into Mitch at the mall a while back and he couldn't stop singing your praises. He mentioned that you were working on something very special for him."

"Mitch is a good man." I said, not wanting to elaborate on anything of a business nature that Mitch and I've discussed.

I briefly drifted away from my conversation with Sheila and wondered how Mitch and Anita were faring. I'd not seen him at KIF's office yet for his tax return preparation, and hadn't talked to him since he signed up for the energy investment. I'm sure by now he would have to say something to Anita about the investment, since it will be appearing on their return. I need to call him soon.

"So do you want to come?" Sheila asked. "Raven…" she yelled.

"Huh?" I said, regaining my attention to the conversation.

"Girl, what is wrong with you? I've asked you three times do you want to come and you've said nothing!" Sheila said, somewhat annoyed.

"I'm sorry girl. I zoned out for a few. Come where?"

"I said that I was going out on Friday night with a few friends to a party. Do you want to come with us?"

"Sure." I said without hesitation. "I need a break from this shit."

"Good. By then I'll have a few properties listed for you to look over."

"Sounds good Sheila." I said appreciatively. "Thanks."

"No problem honey."

Friday couldn't have come soon enough. Sheila called me during the day to tell me that she'd pick me up around 10 p.m., but I declined her ride offer. I like to leave a party when I'M ready to leave and not having to wait for a consensus from the occupants in the car. I got the address from her and told her that I'd meet her there. When I arrived at around 10:30 p.m., I found her and her girls already there.

"Raven", Sheila yelled.

I looked in the direction of the familiar voice, waved, and walked over to meet everyone. Sheila introduced me to Angel, Candice, Barbara, and Rosemary. We made small talk and watched the door periodically to see if any interesting men would arrive. I found out that the party was actually a house warming for a friend of Candice's, Bubbajune.

The lure for Sheila was the fact that Bubbajune, was a police officer. Sheila LOVES men who're involved in law enforcement; therefore, her reasoning was that there should be a shit-load of cops stopping through. She was right. The pickings were very plentiful!

I danced with this one guy whose breath made me suicidal, and when I returned to the couch where all of us had been conversing earlier, no one was there. I couldn't find any of the girls. I began walking around the house looking at Bubbajune's artwork. I began dreaming of my own house and imagined this house being mine and how I'd decorate it.

"K-Mart, $19.95." a voice whispered in my ear.

I turned around and looked into the face of a short, dark-complexioned guy.

"Pardon me?" I asked. Were you talking to me?"

"I certainly was." he said smiling. "the painting came from K-Mart, and it costs $19.95."

"You're good." I said, returning the smile. "...And this vase... what would be your best guess at that?" I said, pointing to a vase sitting on a table.

"Oh, I say garage sale, circa yesterday."

We laughed.

"Hi, I'm Lawton, the owner of the house."

"Bubbajune?" I said smiling. "Are you and he one and the same?"

"That we are, my little pretty." he said in a bad wicked witch from the Wizard of Oz voice.

"My name is Raven."

"Nice to meet you Raven. Who did you come with?" he asked.

"Well, I came alone, but I was invited by Sheila.

"Sheila?"

"Yeah, she's a friend of Candice's."

"Ah yes, Candice." he said as acknowledgement of knowing her. "Where is she?"

"I don't know. Everyone has abandoned me."

"Well, try some of the other floors. There's lots going on all over the house." he said.

"O.K." I said.

Just then, someone in one of the other rooms called out his name.

"Coming!" he responded "Sorry Raven. I've gotta run, but please make yourself at home… and don't forget to check the basement. Movies!"

"Thanks Lawton." I said.

"Please, call me Bubbajune." he said. "All of my friends do."

We both smiled.

"What a nice guy." I thought. "I'm glad that I came."

I took Bubbajune's advice and freely made my way around the house. He was right, there were a lot of things happening. A makeshift firing range was even set up in the attic for pellet and bb-gun practice. I gravitated toward the basement, however, and watched the remainder of a movie already in progress. Bubbajune had provided bowls of popcorn and coke, to give the feeling of being in an actual theater. From the light of the projector, I spied a vacant space on one of the couches. I made my way over there and sat down in between a man on one side and a woman on the other. I hated to be boxed in the middle, but I guess I didn't have much of a choice, being late and all. When the movie ended, the lights came on while the projector was being readied for the next movie. During this "intermission", I turned to the woman to ask her some questions that puzzled me about the previous movie, but just as I turned to face her, she got up from the couch and walked out of the room. The timing couldn't have been more synchronized. I must've had a pretty surprised expression on my face because the guy that remained on the couch with me began laughing. He laughed so hard that it made me laugh too.

"I'm sorry." the man apologized, still laughing a little. "I didn't mean to laugh at you."

"Oh that's O.K." I said. "It was rather funny."

The man extended his hand to me.

"Hi," he said, "my name is Nick."

We shook hands.

"Hi Nick. I'm raven." I said smiling.

"Hi Raven." he said smiling back. "Did you enjoy the movie?" he asked.

"Yeah, what little I got to see, but I don't understand the significance of the broach?"

Nick proceeded to make things clearer for me, filling in all the parts of the movie that I'd missed. Nick's voice was very calming, his smile was very relaxed, but his eyes... Nick's eyes were almost frightening... intense... probing. It would be my guess that he's a detective or something like that. We remained seated next to one another as the next movie began to play. By this time, I'd forgotten all about looking for Sheila and the girls, but unfortunately they hadn't forgotten about me.

"There you are!" Sheila exclaimed. "I've been looking all over for you."

The people toward the front of the room turned around to see who was creating the disturbance. She sat down in the vacant seat on the couch and continued her conversation, however now at a whisper.

"We were thinking about leaving and going to a club."

"We?" I asked.

"Yeah... me, Noah, Landa, Marcia, Kelly, Vinnie, Nay, Peanut..."

I smiled, knowing that Sheila had struck again!

"Thanks for the invite, but I think I'll watch the end of the movie then go home."

Sheila's eyes quickly looked over toward Nick, who was still looking at the movie very intently. She raised her hand toward my face and pinched my cheek, just like a visiting relative would do a child.

"I understand sweetie." she said smiling. "You just run along home."

She stood up to walk away, took a few steps toward the door, then came back.

"Speaking of home, I almost forgot."

She reached into her huge suitcase of a purse and pulled out several folded sheets.

"I've put an asterisk beside the ones that I think would be best for you. There are about thirteen for you to choose from."

"Thanks Sheila."

"Call me later so that we can discuss 'em."

"O.K." I said, and with that she was gone.

Nick turned his head away from the movie and looked at me, smiled, then turned back toward the screen.

"What was that look about?" I thought.

Again I suppose that my facial expression communicated what my mind was thinking and what my mouth refused to say. As he looked at the screen, he said that he was glad that I stayed.

"Oh yeah, why is that?" I asked.

"Because it's about to get good." he said smiling.

I smiled in return.

"The movie?" I asked, feeling that he had something else in mind.

He put his arm around the back of the couch, near the nape of my neck and turned his face from the screen again to look at me.

"Yeah, that too."

Chapter 19:

Home ownership is wonderful! After several months of searching, viewing, submitting contracts, and waiting, I've succeeded! Aside from my KIF apartment, this marks the first time that I've lived alone. Before, there has always been family, roommates, Jerome's parents, and of course Parker. Parker... he seems so far away from where my life is now.

I received several house-warming gifts, but the one that was the most precious to me was from Nick. He gave me a cute little German Shepherd puppy that I named Dick, after Nick's profession (really!). Nick says that he knew that I would get all the customary house-warming gifts from my friends. He was right. Dick is such a wonderful companion for me; greeting me at the door at the end of my work day, wagging his tail. He somehow manages to always put a smile on my face. What a breath of fresh air!

The tax season has come and gone, but instead of having a lull in our service, we've received an extraordinary amount of complaints. There seems to be serious tax flaws with the Energy Investment. The IRS has stepped up its efforts in pressuring our clients about tax exemptions that KIF had guaranteed they were qualified for, so they in turn come into the office very irate, and justifiably so. Instead of a few clients trickling in, as was the case a few months ago when Mr. Higgenbotham was having his problems, they now pour in. Literally fifty to sixty people a day! The situation has now grown so serious that it seems all of our time is devoted to damage control. Wayland's office is constantly occupied with clients who insist on speaking to him personally to address their concerns. I must admit, that he does a good job in calming them down and explaining KIF's position, reassuring them that the correct procedures were adhered to.

"You all must understand that this is the way the IRS operates. You are doing exactly what they want you to do... panic." Wayland would say to the clients. "They know that I am privy to their loopholes; their trade secrets! Afterall, I was once one of THEM, but I broke from their ranks to have my own. They never forgave me for that."

Wayland would talk to these people as if they were children, flailing his arms and pointing his fingers into their faces as though he were chastising them.

"I use their rules to play their game, and to be quite candid with you all, it's the same rules that the White man has been using for years to succeed in this great U.S. of A. Now is the time for US to make those economic strides. I know their 'bible', the Master Tax Guide, like the back of my hand, and they are aware of this. So, don't give them the satisfaction of being intimidated when you're threatened with an audit, or show fear when they want to review your records. Let 'em! They won't find ANYTHING, because there is nothing to FIND! All of your work is in order and is guaranteed and backed by KIF, and as I'm sure all of you know, KIF represents all of our clients in audits or any disputes with the government. Therefore, don't worry about their deadlines and posturing and idle threats. KIF will handle everything for you!"

It was incredible to see the transformation of these angry people being changed into sympathetic Wayland supporters.

"Basically people", he'd say in summary, "all I'm attempting to do is to get US a piece of the pie before it's all eaten. Let me do this for you, let KIF do this for US!"

The man was like a magician with these people. This seemed to be enough to satisfy them, and until they receive some other type of communication from the IRS, they were quite pleased with KIF and its handling of their finances.

Nick and I have been spending a considerable amount of time together since meeting at Bubbajune's house. Nick, whose real name is Nicholas Allen, is about forty years old and has been a member of the Atlanta police force for fourteen years. He got married while attending Maryland University and fathered a daughter. Unfortunately Nick's marriage didn't survive the demands of a growing family. They divorced and he moved to Atlanta, joining the police force. Nick worked his way up from foot patrolman to detective. I knew those probing eyes would reveal something like this; a detective!

I could tell that Nick liked me a lot. About once a week, he would want to get together with me to do something; either go to the movies, to dinner, a sporting event, a musical show, something! I think that I provided him with some degree of balance... and for that matter, he did for me too. We were both so work-driven that our lives didn't leave much room for others.

One day Nick invited me to have lunch with him, but his invitation sounded different to me than his usual requests. This one sounded serious; business.

"Nick," I asked him over the telephone, "are you alright? Is everything O.K?"

Sidestepping my question, Nick responded, "I'll pick you up around one o'clock Raven, O.K? Bye."

He didn't even wait for me to agree when he so abruptly hung up the telephone. I knew that something was troubling my friend.

The restaurant was very crowded with the lunch-time customers. The only seats available were located at the bar, which, in Nick's state of mind, suited him just fine.

"What can I get you folks today?" the bartender asked.

"I'll take a double shot of scotch." Nick replied.

"And I'll have a Baileys on the rocks please." I said.

Nick wouldn't reveal any details to me on the ride to the restaurant, and it drove me nuts! He said that he'd fill me in when we get there. Well, now was that moment.

"Nick, what is wrong? Has something happened to your child? Your job? What?" I asked, unable to stand not knowing any longer.

"Raven, I don't know how to tell you this."

"Tell me what Nick?" I asked in a panic-stricken voice.

Nick raised his glass to his lips and took a hard swallow.

"Raven... Raven..."

"Nick, please! I interrupted. "Just say it."

"You are under arrest. You have the right to remain silent. Anything you say can and will be used against you in a court of law. You have the right…"

"Very funny Nick." I said angrily. "I'm not in the mood for games."

"Raven, I need to tell you something very important, something very sensitive."

I just stared at him, not responding in any way, but he was scaring me now.

"If this information is, in any way, leaked out prematurely, a lot of people could be hurt. Do you understand what I'm saying?"

I'd never seen Nick's face look as serious as it did then.

"O.K. Nick," I said, realizing the level of seriousness.

"Three weeks ago, I sat in on a meeting where I was assigned a case that involves your boss," he said. "Raven, Wayland is not at all the man you think he is."

"Excuse me?" I said with confusion.

"Wayland Hunter is under investigation."

"What?" I asked, surprised. "For what?"

"Fraud, for starters."

I was speechless, my mouth agape.

"There must be some mistake Nick. Wayland has been helping people on their taxes and investments for years. If he were doing something illegal, the government would've stepped in a long time ago, right?"

Nick took another drink from his glass.

"Look Raven, I was just given control of this operation. I've been commanded to bring Hunter and his conspirators to justice."

He finished his drink and called for the bartender to bring him another round.

"You have no idea what I've been going through, trying to appeal to my colleagues and superiors not to move forward on plan A.

Nick rubbed his forehead with his hand in a worrisome motion.

"I'm almost afraid to ask," I said, "but what is plan 'A'?"

Nick took another drink from his glass.

"Plan A involves the arrest of all KIF employees… and that includes you, baby."

I gulped and took a huge swig of my drink, emptying the glass. My brow ruffled and tears filled my eyes. I, too, called for the bartender to bring me another round. My head began to swirl.

"Nick, you gotta know that I have nothing to do with fraud." I exclaimed. "I could never be a party to scamming people out of their savings!"

"I hear what you're saying Raven, but I'm going to need you to come downtown with me."

"You don't believe me?" I said, the tears openly running down my cheeks.

Nick put his arm around me and handed me his handkerchief in his jacket pocket.

"This is very difficult for me too honey." He said. "I begged to be reassigned off of this case, until I heard about the employee roundup. I couldn't just sit by and let that happen to you." Nick said, smiling gently. "But, …"

"There's ALWAYS a 'but'. I interjected.

"…someone has to be accountable." Nick continued.

"Me, right?" I asked.

Nick turned his head away from me and looked into space.

"You need to come downtown to be briefed on the specifics of your assignment."

"What?" I exclaimed, disbelieving this whole thing. "Look Nick, if this case is as serious as you're making it out to be, I don't want to be in the middle playing 'Mission Impossible'!" I said.

"Sweetie, you don't understand. You don't have a choice."

My head was spinning like a top.

"What if I just quit KIF, Nick… just leave the company… leave the area?"

"Then you'll have to endure the humiliation of being tracked down, arrested, and dragged back down here."

"On what grounds? I haven't done anything!", I said adamantly.

"I know that! I believe you, but didn't you participate in his recruitment campaigns?"

"Yes, but…"

"And aren't you the one who signed off on the paperwork for collecting the money during this 'campaign'?"

"Yes Nick, but…"

"And weren't you, up until recently, living in an apartment that was subsidized by these client's money?"

"Wait a second Nick!" I said. "You act as though I'm on trial; as though I have something to hide."

"All I'm trying to do is show you how tainted you could appear if you were before a jury." Nick said.

I was silent.

"Listen sweetheart."

Nick gently touched my face with the palm of his hand.

"Whether you want it to be this way or not, you ARE implicated very deeply in this shit. You ARE involved."

We soon left the restaurant and Nick drove me back to my office. I told him that I would let my staff know that I'm taking off for the rest of the day and that I'd go to the precinct with him.

"Oh, Ms. McNair." Diane said as I walked into the office, "Mr. Hunter called for you about twenty minutes ago. He said to tell you to give him a call as soon as possible.

"Thanks Diane", I said, and proceeded to walk into my office.

I closed the door behind me, sat down at my desk, and cried quietly to myself. I began to think of my friends that I'd talked into getting involved with KIF and the amount of money they'll be losing. I began to think of Mr. Higgenbotham and all the other 'Mr. Higgenbothams' that will probably lose every nickel to their names because of Wayland Hunter's greed, and I began to think of me and the deception that enticed me to his bed. I was sick.

"I wondered how many of KIF's staff is involved in this? What about my secretary? Could she be?" I asked myself. "From this moment on," I thought, "I trust NO ONE!"

I knew that I'd have to conduct myself as I did before I went to lunch; as if I knew nothing of the investigation, so I returned Wayland's call.

"Hi Wayland." I said, trying to sound normal. "You called?"

"Yes I did Raven." Wayland said.

My skin crawled with disdain for him.

"I'll need to get your figures for the quarterly report. Can you stop by my office this evening?"

"Well actually Wayland, I just returned from lunch and I believe that I ate something that didn't agree with me." I said. "I just stopped in to the office to tell my staff that I'm taking the rest of the day off."

"Oh, I'm sorry to hear that Raven. Is there something that I can do to help?"

"Yes motherfucker," I thought, "you can give those innocent people back their money."

"No, nothing. Thanks anyway. I probably just need some rest."

"Well, what about the figures? You know it's due in the morning, and don't forget our staff meeting at 8 a.m. tomorrow morning." Wayland said.

"I'll have Marcus drop off the figures today, and no, I hadn't forgotten about the meeting."

"Fine." he said. "And Raven…"

"Yes."

"…feel better."

"Thanks Wayland." I said.

I hung up the phone and starred into space.

"Yeah Wayland, thanks… for nothing."

Chapter 20:

It was very late when I arrived back home from the precinct. After being questioned for nearly nine hours by the detectives, Nick returned me to my car, which was still parked at the KIF office. I refused Nick's offer to drive me home, still pretty dazed by all the day's excitement. Actually, I didn't care to be in his company right now... anybody's for that matter. I just couldn't believe this was real.

"Ring, ring, ring".

My telephone was ringing off the hook. I raced toward the phone and answered it.

"Hello". I said in a hurried tone.

"Hi sweetie, I was just about to hang up."

It was Darlene. She somehow seems to always call me just when I need to talk to her the most.

"Is this Mayor McNair?" I asked smiling.

"Not yet kiddo... not yet." she said. "You know, I've tried reaching you on your cell AND at your home, but..."

"I know, I know. It's been an insane day here. I've been sorta out of commission."

"Well, look honey." Darlene said, "I was calling to let you know that the election is in a few days, and I was hoping that you would be able to come home to be with me. Can you?"

If only Darlene knew. If only I could share this with her. I would love nothing more than to escape this lunacy and be with my family, but I can't... not now.

134

"Sorry, now is not a good time for me." I said, with a lump in my throat.

"Raven, you've got to take some time off from work, honey." Darlene advised. "This isn't very healthy."

"I know, I know. I will as soon as I can."

"Well, say your prayers for me." Darlene said. "A few more days will determine my next four years."

I thought to myself, "me too", but said aloud, "You know my prayers are with you always. I could use your prayers too, Sis."

"You got it." Darlene replied. "Oh, by the way," Darlene said, I got the pictures you sent of the new house and of Dick. I especially liked the one of Dick chasing you across your yard."

"Yeah, he is a cutie pie, isn't he?"

"He sure is, and your house is beautiful. I can't wait to see it for myself."

"Call me the moment you know the outcome of the election."

"I will. I love you." she said.

And with that, she was gone.

Earlier, Jerome was good enough to stop by my house and let Dick outside to relieve himself in the backyard. I kicked off my shoes, and laid across the living room couch, exhausted. I couldn't focus on anything! I replayed the the experience of what I just endured over and over in my mind.

Nick and his three colleagues wanted to know about Wayland's comings and goings, his bank accounts, KIF's bank holdings, especially the one he has in Switzerland, Wayland's friends and any personal information, any family members that I'm aware of, his real estate, his travels, which includes the trip to the Caribbean, any wealthy clients that he is particularly close to... EVERYTHING!

"Ms. McNair," I recall detective Jimmy saying to me, "Mr. Hunter has been under investigation for some time now."

"How long is 'some time'?" I asked. "Weeks, months?"

"Nine years", another detective replied.

"Nine years?" I said in outrage. "Why hasn't he been arrested by now? Why are you taking so long to do what's right?"

"Ms McNair," the detective tried to interject, but I continued. "Are you aware of how many people he has lured into this diabolical trap while you guys just observe? Old people, young people, everyone losing their life savings while you're at a window somewhere looking through binoculars!" I said, my arms flailing.

"Calm down Raven." Nick said.

"Calm down?" I said defiantly. "This is partly YOUR fault! You guys let it continue! Had you done your jobs, then I, nor the other honest people who work at KIF would have never MET the man! He would've been in jail!" I said, my voice growing louder with anger.

"O.K. Nick", another detective said as he walked briskly toward Nick, I've had just about enough of her mouth."

"EVERYONE CLAM DOWN!" Nick shouted.

Nick looked toward the perturbed detective.

"C'mon Curtis, sit down… please."

The detective reluctantly walked back over to his seat. Nick looked toward me.

"Look Raven, our department is so stretched to the limit; a few people to do the work of many. So calm it down a bit."

"Fine Nick," I said, "but I've just been HIT with this bombshell! My life feels as though it is crumbling and I've not been able to sort this thing through."

"Well that's not your job to sort it through, not is it Ms. McNair?" detective Curtis said in a sarcastic tone.

"I can't win in this room." I thought.

"Hold on Curtis." one of the other detectives said. "There's no cause to attack her any further."

"You guys need to wake the fuck up!" detective Curtis shouted. "She is knee deep in this shit, and as far as I'm concerned, she probably helped Hunter mastermind that last scam."

"What last scam?" I asked perplexed. "I'm not a part of any scams… past, present, or future!"

"Sure you aren't." detective Curtis said in disbelief.

"Curtis, you know that theory has been disproved by our insider, so get off of that shit." Nick said.

"Insider?" I said. "Like a spy? Like a plant?"

Again Curtis rose from his chair and walked right up to my face, pointing his finger very close to my nose. I guess this was his way of trying to intimidate me. It worked.

"You know what honey, you watch too much damn t.v." detective Curtis said. "Wake up, this is the real world."

The room was quiet for a few seconds. The tension of it all made me break down and cry. Detective Curtis walked away from me, to the other side of the room. Nick began pacing, then walked over to me and sat on top of the long table with his foot on my chair. Tears were streaming down my face uncontrollably.

"Raven," Nick said. "I'm sorry that you are involved in this..."

"But I'm not involved in this... I'm innocent Nick." I said sobbing.

"Well innocent or not, this is only the beginning." one other detective said.

"What did that mean, 'only the beginning'?" I thought. I decided that I wouldn't add anything to the conversation, for fear of detective Curtis' reprisal, and although Nick was here and I trusted him, I'd not yet spoken with an attorney.

"We understand from our man inside that Wayland keeps all of KIF's records in one central location in his office. Is that correct?" detective Jimmy asked.

"I'm not sure." I replied.

"What ARE you sure about, Ms. McNair? What DO you know?" detective Curtis said.

I didn't respond, instead I looked toward Nick.

"Raven," Nick said, "we'll need for you to gain access into Wayland's inner office and recover some documents for our investigation. I will show you how to use the lock picking instruments and..."

"Wait a minute damnit!" I said, refusing to hold my tongue any longer. You're asking me to put my life in danger."

"You are already facing the possibility of a jail sentence, Ms. McNair." detective Curtis said. "Your life is already in jeopardy."

This was the first factual thing that this asshole has spoken all day. He was right. I have to clear my name and rebuild the trust of my friends and family: Jerome and his parents, Sheila, Calvin, Elliott,

Mitch and Anita, Mr. Alvin, everyone! This is a mess! How do I show my innocence and restore my integrity? By helping to uncover Wayland's elaborate scam and bring his sorry ass to justice. He must pay. He WILL pay!

Chapter 21:

"...and let me say in conclusion that I am very proud of each and every one of you." Wayland said. "Everyone stand and give yourselves a hand for an outstanding job for YOUR company, KIF".

Everyone did as was instructed, smiling and patting one another on the back in celebration. The meeting had more of a pep-rally flavor than that of a staff meeting. Wayland stood at the front of the office, flanked by two of his three departmental heads, Victoria and Paul. Each one, in turn, made a speech about their groups' specific gains during the quarter and what their particular tax shelter could expect to generate for the upcoming period. When it was time for Richard, the head of the third group, to tell of his group's progress, the update was given by Tony. Although Tony was Richard's top-producing agent, why didn't Richard speak for himself. After all, he WAS present. When Tony was done with his presentation, we all learned of the reason.

"I've noticed a number of perplexed looks throughout the room, and you're probably asking yourselves why was Tony representing the group and not Richard himself? Well, after extensive conversations with Richard, he has decided that he'd like to spend more time traveling and seeing the world. So let us all put our hands together to wish Richard happiness in his new endeavors."

"Must be nice!" someone shouted from the back of the room.

Everyone laughed, except Richard.

"Therefore," Wayland continued, "who am I to stand in his way? We were fortunate that Tony has agreed to head Richard's department, and keep things moving forward without a considerable disruption to the group. Thank you Tony for your service."

Everyone applauded. Some even came to the front of the room to pat Tony on the back and to shake hands with a seated, solemned-faced Richard.

"If a man has decided that he could travel and 'see the world', as Wayland puts it," I thought, "then why isn't he smiling? Something more than meets the eye is happening."

Gladys, who was seated next to me, whispered something to me about Wayland finally waking up. I didn't respond, and just kept clapping as the others did.

"If only she knew". I thought. "We are the ones who're asleep."

The following evening after work, I went to the main office, figuring that practically everyone would be gone. I sat at one of the temporary work stations and pretended to do paperwork. I don't remember what I thought I could accomplish that night, but I felt that I had to start somewhere, trying to gather something. There were about eight other people remaining in the office. Some were making telephone calls, some worked at their computers, and still others chatted amongst themselves about the information they've heard throughout the day. Listening to them, I couldn't help but think of how devastating their lives will become when this charade is totally exposed. Wayland has convinced them that their work is so important, that they've all become so driven to make more and more money for KIF, thus more money for themselves. I felt so sorry for them, at least the innocent ones. But how could I tell the 'good guys' from the 'bad guys'? Again, as I'd thought before, proceed with caution and trust no one.

It was now approaching ten o'clock. Everyone had gone except for one person, Victoria's personal secretary. I could see her in the upstairs offices, so I could keep an unobstructed watch on her and would know when she's leaving. As I sat at my work station, I thought that what I needed to do first was to gain quick entry into Wayland's office. Once inside, I could take my time and search around. I also thought of the lock picking techniques that Nick taught me. Because Wayland's office remains locked at all times, I knew that I would get my chance at using the tools tonight.

"You're working rather late tonight." Vera said as she passed my work station, fumbling to put on her coat.

"Yeah, this work seems to never go away." I said as a 'cover'.

"Well Raven, I hate to have to leave you here all alone, but I've got to go."

"No apologies necessary Vera. I shouldn't be that much longer myself."

"Well, lock up tight, and BE CAREFUL. This place gives me the creeps at night."

"Thank you. I will."

We both said goodnight to one another, then my real work began. I waited about twenty   minutes after she left, just to make sure that she wouldn't double back for any reason. I wanted to take as few chances as possible. Reaching into my purse, I removed a small leather case containing the lock picking tools and ascended the spiral, metal staircase. At the top of the stairs, I motioned to the right and entered through the double glass doors into Gwen's office. Everything was rather dark, with the exception of the light emitting from her computer monitor, where a screen-saver program was running. Soon after, I was to hear the sounds that Nick had taught me to listen for; click… click… click. The tumblers had fallen in the lock. I did it! I turned the knob and quickly moved inside, closing the door behind me. I let out a sigh of relief, because I was scared to death and very proud of myself for achieving this feat. The blinds were already drawn in his office and, like Gwen's computer monitor, Wayland's monitor was running the same screen-saver program. It provided me with enough light to get to his file cabinets.

"Damn!" I said, discovering that all the drawers were locked. I tried another, and another, but like the first, they too were locked. I began to perspire profusely now, feeling defeated. I decided that I'll try one more location before I left for the night.

"There must be something in or around his desk that would be useful to the investigation." I thought.

I turned around to walk to the desk, when I noticed a red LED light blinking in the upper corner of the room behind the door. It immediately brought to mind the blinking red light that I saw on the yacht in Jamaica. I couldn't think about that right now for too long.

I needed to do what I had to do and GET OUT! No sooner had I taken three steps toward the desk, did Wayland's desk light come on. My heart pounded with such force that I literally rocked with each heartbeat.

"What do you call yourself doing, sweet thang?" I was asked.

I was speechless, startled beyond words.

"I'll ask you again… what the FUCK are you doing in here rummaging through this office?"

"I… I…" I replied, no knowing what to say.

What could I say? That I'm here spying for the police to find evidence against KIF? Richard took a drink from his almost empty bottle of vodka and reared back in Wayland's chair.

"Well, well, well. Now ain't this interesting." Richard said in a very smug tone.

"Richard, what are YOU doing in here?" I finally managed to say.

"Let me get this straight. YOU break in here, and you want to question ME?"

He broke out in wild laughter.

"Any good employee would get on the phone right now and report this shit immediately to Wayland."

He picked up the handset of the telephone. My body shook with terror.

"But as I said, you'd have to be a good employee."

He then slammed down the telephone receiver.

"I mean, to the untrained eye," Richard continued, "it looks at though you're spying; but I guess to the trained eye, hell, it still looks like you're spying!"

Richard burst into wild laughter again, and lifted the bottle to his lips to take another drink. The smile on his face quickly disappeared, as Richard began to cry.

"But fuck it! FUCK HIM! That lying, double-crossing murderer."

"What?" I screamed inside to myself.

Considering Richard's present state, did he mean 'murderer' as in Wayland murdered his career, or was this said and meant as in a body? A corpse? What have I stumbled upon? If I thought I was scared before, I certainly was now. Richard took another drink from his bottle.

"Richard, what do you mean 'murderer'?" I asked.

Ignoring my question, Richard was on his own drunken train of thought.

"You lying son-of-a-bitch! This all could've been mine! It should've been mine! What about your promise of financial security for the rest of my miserable, motherfuckin' life!"

Richard stood up as best he could, pounding with his fist on the desk.

"Now he's DUMPING me, Yvette.

"Yvette?" I thought.

"All that I've done for him. I helped to make all of this possible, and that greedy ingrate is sending ME out to pasture?"

He took another long gulp from his bottle, this time with some spilling out of his mouth and running down his chin. I moved toward one of the two chairs that were in front of Wayland's desk and sat down, stunned by this turn of events.

"So this retirement isn't your decision?" I asked, trying to get more information out of him.

"Hell no! Why would anyone leave a job making three-hundred thousand dollars a year for doing absolutely NOTHING? That bastard owed this to me. I helped him kill MY own flesh and blood for this fuckin' money! I took the sole blame for it. I did the time, not him. I'm the one haunted day and night by ghosts, and quite frankly, I'm tired of running."

Richard took another drink, wiping his mouth with the sleeve of his shirt.

"Do you understand?" Richard asked sadly. "I'm tired of running from the ghosts."

"I understand Richard." I said sympathetically.

"Look, I don't give a fuck why you're here." Richard said in an exhausted voice. "I just want that bastard to pay... to feel a fraction of the pain that he's caused me over the last twenty-five years."

"Well, I have my own bone to pick with him. What can you help me with Richard?" I asked. "What information can you give me to help bring him down?"

"I have everything! I have taped conversations in my home vault of him planning the murder."

"Do you have any keys to the KIF files? Do you know where Wayland keeps the keys to these files?" I said pointing to the cabinets.

"He's much too clever to leave the keys here. No one has access to his files. Wayland's important documents are kept in his home, this I know for sure. That shit over there..."

He pointed to the metal cabinets in the office.

"I wouldn't be surprised if all of the drawers held bricks!"

He laughed, then took his last drink of the vodka.

"Richard! Listen to me! This is very important! Can you give me ANY inside information about KIF, Inc.?"

Richard smiled.

"I have Swiss bank account numbers, I have names of fictitious people and numbers of safe deposit boxes, dummy corporations that he's funneling money through... I got everything!"

"Will you work with me, Richard? Can I count on you to supply me with this information?" I pleaded.

Richard looked me squarely in the eyes, his face changing, as if he'd instantly become cold sober.

"You come see me tomorrow at my home, 'round 3 p.m." Richard said. "I'll have some shit for you that'll make your pretty little head spin. You'll see."

Chapter 22:

I tossed and turned in my bed for the remainder of the night, unable to believe what had transpired. What began as just a search to obtain information on KIF, has developed into a murder confession.

"MURDER!" I said aloud. Could this be true? It all seemed like a dream; more appropriately, a nightmare! I rolled over in my bed, burrowing my face in the pillow.

"If what Richard said was the truth," I thought, "then why would he not have used this alleged taped murder plot for his own defense. Why was Wayland not implicated and sent to prison, as Richard was? Maybe it was planned so that Richard would be the one to take the fall?" I theorized, "but why?" I had so many questions, and no one to supply their answers, except for the most unlikeliest KIF ally I'd ever think to have. Hopefully, by days end, I too will have the answer.

I turned to my right to look at the clock on the nightstand. Nine o'clock a.m. I still had plenty of time to call Nick and bring him up to date on the situation, but I decided that I'd call after I talked with Richard. Why? I suppose to feel like I triumphed alone in getting information on Wayland.

"Ring, ring, ring!" the telephone sounded. It startled me so, that I literally jumped.

"What if it's Wayland?" I thought. "What would I say? What COULD I say?"

"Ring, ring, ring!"

Again the ring of the phone pierced the silence of my room. I decided that I'd let my answering machine take the call. The machine's outgoing message began as I eagerly awaited the sound of the returning voice. I was relieved to hear that it was Jerome, and immediately picked it up.

"Rome, Rome!" I said in agony, trying to catch him before he hung up the phone.

Hearing the sound of my voice, Jerome asked if everything was alright.

"No… I mean yes… I mean no!" I replied in a confused state.

He invited me to have breakfast with him. This was perfect, because then I could let him know what's been happening. However, in telling him about Wayland and the KIF con, I would also have to reveal to him that his and his parents' investment money may be unrecoverable; that they may have lost their combined principal of thirty thousand dollars. I don't know how he's going to respond to that, but I can only pray that he won't be too unforgiving of me. Afterall, I WAS trying to do the right thing for them, as with all of my friends and family. I hope that he understands this, for my sake.

Jerome arrived at my house an hour later. We decided to eat at Tia's Treasure, a well-known breakfast cafe. During the ride there, I began my account of events of the week. I'd only gotten as far as telling him about Nick revealing the investigation on Wayland and my being questioned in the police station before Jerome pulled the car over to the side of the road. His face was contorted and was visibly disturbed.

"What?" Jerome said in shock.

He now wanted to give me his undivided attention. For a few seconds, he just stared at me. I felt very uncomfortable, like I'd let him down. I looked away from him, as I couldn't bear to see the look of disappointment in his eyes. The only sound that could be heard was the faint sound of Jerome's all-news radio station giving information from around the area. I continued to tell him about everything; the money he'll probably never see again, the undercover work I'm doing for the police, and of course, Richard's admission last night. With his mouth agape, Jerome just looked at me in disbelief, not saying a word.

"So, that brings me to today." I said. "I have a three o'clock appointment with Richard at his house."

"Excuse me?" Jerome said, not wanting to believe what he'd heard. "You're going to see a confessed murderer AT HIS HOUSE?" he yelled. "Are you out of your FUCKING mind Raven?"

I was silent. I knew that Jerome was upset with me, as he had a right to be, but as much as I didn't want to hurt him, I wanted to be instrumental in defeating Wayland more.

"Rome", I said almost pleading, "he has evidence that can…"

"WAIT A MINUTE DAMNIT!" You are WAY in over your head." Jerome said angrily. "Don't you think that this is a matter for the police? After all babe, you're not REALLY a policewoman."

"I'm not trying to act like one." I said defensively. "I just want to GET this guy. I'll call Nick, Rome, I promise that I will, but AFTER I meet with Richard. This meeting is already set up."

"So." Jerome said.

"So, I'm going through with it." I said with more aggression. "Wayland has fucked up so many people's lives, so many hopes dashed."

I thought of Alvin, the old elevator operator. I thought of Mitch and Anita and their baby, and the thousands of people who I'll personally never know .

"I HAVE to do this Rome! I gotta make this right, or at least try."

Neither of us spoke to the other. Jerome faced forward, staring through the windshield with a blank expression on his face. I guess I'd given him too much to digest all at once. Actually, I find myself somewhat overwhelmed too. I've asked myself an endless barrage of questions: What if Richard now denies everything? What if he's sobered up and has told Wayland about ME snooping around in his office? What if the two of them are in wait for my arrival? What if I'm being setup for harm? The questions drive me crazy, but hopefully at 3 o'clock, they can all be answered.

Jerome put the car back in gear and we proceeded to Tia's. As we drove in silence, a news announcement on the radio caught my attention.

"…still authorities have not yet disclosed the identity of the Black male that plunged to his death last night from atop the roof of the Aurora Building." the voice on the radio said. "Sources close to the case say that a note has been recovered from the body and that the death will more than likely be ruled a suicide. However, the case is still under investigation."

My eyes were transfixed on the radio.

"Oh my GOD!" I whispered.

Jerome turned to look at me.

"What?" Jerome asked concerned.

With a look of dread on my face, I wondered aloud if it could be Richard. A panicky feeling came over me. I picked up my cell phone, feeling an urgent need to hear Richard's voice. I needed to know if he was at home preparing for our appointment or at the county morgue. When I dialed, then heard Richard's voice, I was relieved. I merely told him that I was calling to confirm our appointment.

"Oh yeah." Richard said. "I'm looking forward to this."

I could sense that Richard was smiling.

"I've got everything in a manila envelope waiting for you. It's all yours."

"Good." I said. "I'll see you at three."

After eating, Jerome told me that he couldn't, in good conscious, let me go to Richard's house alone. He said that he'd accompany me. He insisted, however, on stopping by his house first to grab a couple of things. Those 'things' turned out to be a .38 caliber gun and a handheld digital recorder. I guess Jerome said it best:

"Look babe, this is reality. This man, Richard, has already admitted to killing someone," he said, "what makes you think that he'll find a moral dilemma in killing us? I'm personally not willing to take that kind of risk."

I rolled the car window down to get some fresh air; to clear my head. I took very deep breaths and wondered whether or not I was, in fact, doing the right thing. We arrived outside of Richard's home about twenty minutes early. To guard against Jerome being detected with the recorder, he thought it best to activate the record mode from inside the car. This way, we could look more 'natural' walking up to the house. When we arrived, we could see that his front door was ajar. We walked up to the door and I called out his name.

"Richard, it's Raven."

No answer.

I knocked and called out for him again. Still no answer. This time I knocked a little harder, intentionally pushing the door open wider, but still I got no response. Jerome and I looked at one another, neither of us not knowing quite what to make of this. With his left hand, Jerome held the micro recorder, his arms comfortably hanging downward. With his right hand, he held the gun inside of his pocket. We returned our attention to the house.

"Raven." Jerome said, his eyes transfixed on something inside. He motioned to the left side of the room with his head.

"Richard!" I gasped.

Richard was lying on the floor in a fetal position. A chair was toppled on the floor behind him. I surmised that he had been sitting there. I entered the house and walked briskly toward him. Jerome reluctantly followed, looking around the room very cautiously. The interior of the house was rather dark, as the drapes over the windows had not been drawn open.

"This guy must have an obsession with clocks," Jerome said, "Look".

Still walking, I looked quickly around the room. Jerome was right. The room was filled with clocks; on the mantle piece, on the tables, on the walls, everywhere! Richard even had a teak grandfather clock situated to one side of the room that stood from floor to ceiling. It was grand, but I couldn't really focus very well on his collection; afterall, he's lying unresponsive on the floor. I must admit, though, the closer I neared Richard, the more fearful I became. I bent over him.

"Richard, Richard!" I yelled, shaking him lightly, but still I got no response.

"From what you told me about this guy, maybe the son-of-a-bitch is drunk." Jerome said, still keeping a watchful eye around the room.

Maybe there was some truth to Jerome's hunch, so I knelt down beside him. I took in a deep breath to perhaps catch a whiff of alcohol, but I didn't detect any.

Maybe he fell out of the chair and hit his head on the floor?" I thought. "Maybe he's …"

I turned my head back to an approaching Jerome.

"Rome," I said in almost a panic, "help me get him up."

Without thinking, Jerome quickly placed the tape recorder on the floor near the toppled chair. He leaned over Richard and turned him over, face up.

"DAMN!" Jerome exclaimed.

Richard had what appeared to be a bullet wound to the chest. Jerome felt his neck to find out if a pulse still existed.

"C'mon, let's get out of here babe." Jerome said, pulling me up from the floor. "This man is dead. We can call the police from my car."

I looked very quickly around the immediate area to see if I saw the manila envelope that Richard had spoken of earlier, but I didn't see it.

"Shit!" I said, as Jerome and I ran toward the door.

"Raven, don't touch anything, not even the door knob." Jerome said. "I'll swing the door closed with my foot."

"Poor Richard." I said, now with tears streaming down my face.

Jerome pulled the door ajar, as we found it. We quickly got into the car and sped away.

As Jerome's car moved further down the street and disappeared from view, Wayland released his hold of the edge of the window curtain.

"Damn that prying bitch!" Wayland muttered, "and damn you, Richard!" he shouted in Richard's direction.

Wayland, who had just moments earlier sought refuge inside of Richard's closet to remain undetected by Raven and Jerome, now freely walked about.

"You just had to be a smart-ass, didn't you Richard. You had to push things to the limit." Wayland shouted. "I didn't want to have to take you out like this, but you asked for it… you useless, drunken fool."

Wayland removed a gun from the waist of his pants. He unscrewed the silencer on the end of the barrel and began wiping the weapon off with a handkerchief, removing all evidence of his fingerprints.

"What was it that made you THINK that you could outwit ME? You're not in my league. And then to try and blackmail ME?" Wayland said, hitting his chest with his open hand. "If you weren't already dead, I'd shoot your monkey ass again!

Wayland bent down towards Richard and placed the gun in his hand, squeezing Richard's fingers around the handle and his index finger on the trigger.

"This'll be a nice, neat picture for the police to find, and when they ask me about you, I'll simply say that you became very depressed about your sudden career move. You even spoke to me about suicide", Wayland said smiling, "but how was I to know that you would ACT on it?"

Wayland began laughing as he walked around the room.

"I guess you won't be needing this anymore."

He waved the manila envelope in the air.

"You see all the trouble that THIS has caused?" he continued.

Wayland placed the envelope under his arm.

"If only you could've learned to keep your fucking mouth shut," Wayland lectured, "this could've all been avoided. No one needed to know SHIT about me! NO ONE, including that bitch Raven! But it's all good. I've got something special lined up for her ass."

Wayland walked toward the back door of the house, just as he'd entered. He turned around to admonish Richard one last time.

"You talked one time too many Richard, you drunken bastard! I had to close that mouth of yours once and for all."

The alarm on the grandfather clock began to chime. Three bells rang out, filling the room. Wayland closed the door shut, leaving his brother-in-law dead on the floor, and Jerome's recorder, recording it all.

Chapter 23:

After leaving Richard's home, Jerome pulled into a nearby gas station and, shaking nervously, I telephoned Nick's office. Surprisingly, I got someone other than Nick.

"I'm sorry", the voice on the other end of the receiver said, "the detective isn't in the office right now. May I help you?"

"I'm calling to report an officer down." I lied, thinking that would make the police respond faster.

"What did you say ma'am?" Would you repeat that message?" the man asked.

"OFFICER DOWN, OFFICER DOWN!" I yelled.

I gave the person Richard's address very quickly. As I was hanging up the phone, I could hear him ask my name. I hung up, not wanting to become any more entangled in this mess than I already am.

I was devastated. I had Jerome drive me to my place to pick up Dick and to pack a small suitcase of clothing. I left with him heading for his house, and for the next few days, I didn't have any contact with anyone. Quite naturally, I didn't want to go to KIF, and even more so I didn't want to face Wayland; not right now. Although I had no proof, I know within my heart that he killed Richard. Jerome suggested that I go home, that is, back to Iowa for a break from all of this. Inasmuch as I would love to see my family, I couldn't with any consciousness leave. I had to try and make justice work, for the sake of all the people he stole from, including me.

On the third day of staying with Jerome, I felt better and stronger. I called my voice mail to check my messages. Oddly enough, no one from KIF called to check on me, not even MY secretary. I found that to be quite strange. I called Jerome at work and told him about it, but he said it sounded like nothing to be alarmed about.

"Was I becoming paranoid?" I thought.

Following my instinct, I called into my office.

"Good morning," Diane said in a pleasant voice, "KIF Financial Group."

"Diane, this is Ms. McNair."

The phone was silent.

"Diane, are you still there? Do you hear me?"

"Ms. McNair, this is an unexpected surprise."

"Unexpected?" I thought. Why would calling into MY OWN OFFICE be considered as a surprise?"

"Why so, Diane?" I asked.

"I'm sorry Ms. McNair, but I can't talk to you. Please understand."

"What is going on Diane? Has something been said about me?" I asked puzzled.

"I'm sorry Ms. McNair. I liked you as a boss, and I'm sure you must've had a good reason for doing what you did, but you must turn yourself in to the authorities." she said. "It's not worth it."

"Excuse me?" I said confused.

And with that, Diane hung up the telephone.

"What the fuck was that conversation all about?" I asked myself.

I decided that I'd take a shower, get dressed, and go to KIF to confront Wayland. I called Jerome but got his voice mail. I left him a message that I was going to the office. In lieu of all that has transpired, I felt much more secure in having someone know where I am at all times, and what better person than Jerome. To get a better understanding of what I'd be walking into, I called the main office of KIF to try and connect with Elizabeth.

"Raven, what in the hell do you think you're doing?" she whispered, evidently not wanting anyone to know that she was talking to me. "Please, tell me that it's not true."

"Slow down Elizabeth. That's what I'm calling you for." I said. "What the fuck is going on?"

"You're asking me?" Elizabeth said.

"What's being said?" I asked, slightly losing my patience.

"It was announced in the morning meeting that you have embezzled money from the company."

"I was afraid of that." I said. "He's now trying to cover his tracks and divert attention away from himself by discrediting me!"

"Well, what's the real story then?" Elizabeth asked.

"You'll find out soon enough". I said in a threatening tone. "I'm on my way to the office."

When I arrived at the KIF office, Elizabeth was waiting for me on the outside. When she saw my car pull up, she ran toward the curb to flag me down.

"Open the door". She said sternly.

As she entered my car, she said that she thought it best for us to go someplace to talk in private first; so that she would be prepared when we go inside of the office. I drove around the corner and parked to the far end of a parking lot. An hour and a half later, I'd explained to her everything! She was also in full support of me confronting Wayland, and said that she'd even go with me, just in case. That made me feel good. She asked had I notified the police about being there today.

"No." I said. "I just want Wayland to know that I know everything and that I'm going to stop this shit, stop him!". I said.

"Well, he's in his office now Raven." Elizabeth said. "Let's go!"

I drove the car back over to the headquarters. Elizabeth and I didn't stop to talk to anyone as we entered the building. Luckily it was around the lunch hour, and very few people were there anyway. There were about three agents talking with clients at their desks, but practically no one was around. I was very afraid as Elizabeth and I made our way up the winding stairway to his office, but I was more determined to nail him than fearing him. Gwen was away from her desk, so we barged right in. Elizabeth slammed the door behind us. He'd evidently already seen us as we entered the building and showed no surprise at all in seeing us.

"I sensed I'd be seeing you soon Raven," Wayland said as he turned to face us, "but I wasn't expecting you for this meeting Elizabeth."

Elizabeth was standing slightly behind me to my right. I felt safer knowing that she was there.

"You cheating son-of-a-bitch! How could you? You've defrauded hundreds of people out of their life savings…"

"I defrauded? No, I invested." he said smiling. "It's not my fault that their investments went sour. That's the chance you take when you play the market."

"You lying piece of shit!" I shouted. "You murdered Richard too."

"I murdered no one!" Wayland yelled back at me. "Richard killed himself. I think they call that suicide."

Wayland laughed. I felt the anger boil over inside of me.

"You know, I don't know what I was thinking of in coming here today. Maybe hoping that you still had some sliver of decency inside of you to perhaps turn yourself in."

As I was talking, Wayland walked toward one of his tv monitors.

"Well, if I turn myself in, I'd surely have to implicate my partner who was instrumental in every aspect of this scheme." he said smiling.

He pushed play on the dvd player that was positioned below the monitor.

"So, as you see, you also have a lot riding here. Get it? Riding here". He let out a frightening maniacal laugh.

My heart sank. I felt that I'd been slapped across my face with a two by four. It was me and Wayland making love on the ship during the Jamaican trip.

"Oh my GOD." I whispered.

"Raven? Is that you?" Elizabeth asked, then began joining in the laughter with Wayland.

I turned to look at her and was surprised to find HER pointing a gun at ME!

"You silly little bitch." Elizabeth said. "You think that I'm gonna let you jeopardize all the work that Wayland and I do here?" she said with venom. "I'll KILL you first before I let that happen."

That was the last straw for me. With my sexual exploits still playing on the screen, I tuned out from everything. I felt weak and slumped down on a nearby couch, motionless.

"Why Elizabeth?" I asked, feeling totally defeated. "He murdered Richard! What is it to stop him from murdering you?"

"Well, you know what they say Raven," Elizabeth said smiling, "birds of a feather flock together."

"And do you know what they also say Elizabeth?" I replied, "what's done in the dark will comet to light."

"Enough of what the fuck THEY say!" Wayland said. We don't fear the fuckin' police! By the time they arrive, we'll be long gone."

"But this time, before we leave, we have to take care of a little unfinished business with you, my dear" Elizabeth said.

Just then, a knock was heard on Wayland's door, and a male voice on the other side requested to see him.

"Who is it?" Wayland said impatiently, as he pushed the stop button on the dvd player.

"Don't try to be cute Raven," Elizabeth whispered in my ear, "because nothing would please me more than to shoot your ass. I may get caught, but I'll see that you are dead."

She shoved the gun's barrel into my back, I guess to let me know that she meant business.

"It's Gevan, Wayland. I need for you to meet someone. A prospective client of KIF who could possibly become very important to us". He said proudly.

"Gevan, I'm very busy at the moment. I wished that you'd called me first. Just a moment."

Wayland looked over toward me.

"You open your mouth once, and not only will YOU get it, but those two as well. You understand?" he threatened.

I nodded my head slowly.

Elizabeth had to conceal the gun, so she held it behind the cushion of the couch where I sat. I could still feel the hard barrel against my back and was very much aware that the cushion would in no way deflect a bullet. I sat there in shock, not believing that this is happening. Wayland walked across the room and opened the door. His idea was to talk to Gevan and his guest in the outer office, Gwen's office, but somehow Gevan went around Wayland, and the next thing that I knew, they were all standing in Wayland's office. Very excited and not yet focused on anyone else being in the room, Gevan continued to talk to Wayland.

"Wayland, I'd like for you to meet Nicholas Adoratelli! Mr. Adoratelli, Wayland Hunter."

The two men shook hands, with Wayland facing me and Elizabeth.

"Adoratelli… Adoratelli…" Wayland said. "Where do I know that name?"

"Mr. Adoratelli owns several local malls and the Jerry Jack franchise, Wayland," Gevan chimed in. "He's in the market for some diversity in his investment portfolio, and he's come to KIF for that reason."

"Well that's wonderful!" Wayland said smiling. "You've certainly come to the right place. How much were you thinking of investing, Mr. Adoratelli?" Wayland asked, still smiling. "We have some very attractive strategies right now."

"I was thinking along the lines of an initial investment of five million." The gentleman said. "Is that a figure that you can handle?"

"I'd say so." Wayland said, now grinning from ear to ear.

"That's good Mr. Hunter…"

Please, call me Wayland."

"Alright, Wayland. My thinking is that if this works out successfully, there's more where that came from."

"Wonderful, Mr. Adoratelli. "Why don't we step into one of my colleagues' offices down the hall so that we can find something to your liking." Wayland said.

"And what about your meeting?"

"I'm sure that my associate, Elizabeth, can handle this situation here. Am I right Elizabeth?"

"Absolutely Mr. Hunter." Elizabeth said.

"Raven! Where have you been? I've missed you." Gevan said, finally noticing me in the room.

"I've missed you too Gevan." I said, giving all that I could of a smile.

I truly didn't want to get anyone else shot, but I be damned if I were going to let this opportunity escape me. Gevan walked over to me and I immediately stood up. We hugged one another. Up till now, Mr. Adoratelli's back had been the only thing of the man facing me; however, when he turned around to see who it was that Gevan was hugging, our eyes met. He gave me a very warm and familiar smile. It was Nick; MY Nick!

"Mr. Adoratelli," Gevan said, releasing our embrace, "I'd like for you to meet two other members of our KIF family, my immediate boss, Ms. Raven McNair, and one of jour top agents, Ms. Elizabeth Samuels."

"A pleasure ladies." Nick replied.

He walked over to shake our hands. Elizabeth would now have to drop the gun behind the cushion and I could then move further away from danger. They wouldn't dare to make a scene with so much high-stakes, quick money on the line. I extended my hand to Nick.

"It's very nice to see you … I mean, meet you Mr. Adoratelli." I said stumbling.

"And you, Ms. McNair."

Nick then looked toward Elizabeth and extended his arm toward her to shake her hand.

"Ms. Samuels, is it?"

"Yes, Mr. Adoratelli." Elizabeth said beaming while shaking his hand, "it is my pleasure."

"Well, it'll be interesting to see if you still feel this pleasure tomorrow." Nick said smiling.

"Excuse me?" Elizabeth said. "I don't quite understand what you mean."

"Please, let me rephrase it. You are under arrest Ms. Samuels." Nick said.

Elizabeth tried to pull away from Nick's grasp.

"Nick," I screamed, "she has a gun behind the couch cushions."

"I know." he said, while picking her up and taking her closer to the glass window. He quickly pulled out his handcuffs and cuffed her to a file cabinet. Everything seemed to be moving in slow motion. Wayland hastily made a move to recover what was probably a gun from his desk drawer, but quickly changed his mind.

"I wouldn't if I were you." Gevan said, drawing his handgun on Wayland. "Put your hands above your head and come from behind the desk slowly."

Gevan approached Wayland with handcuffs in one hand, and his gun in the other.

"Are you o.k. Raven?" Nick asked.

I assured him that I was. By this time, I was just trying to stay out of the way. I found refuge standing in a corner of the room with my back against a wall. I was stunned by all that was happening. Never would I have guessed that the undercover cop was Gevan! I guess that explains why he was such a bad salesman.

"What is the meaning of this shit Gevan?" Wayland protested. "Do you want money? Is that it?"

"Yeah, that's exactly what we want Wayland; about eighty million dollars that you've swindled from a lot of innocent people over the years."

"I don't know what you're talking about." Wayland said. "I've never robbed anyone of anything."

"Tell it to the judge." Nick said.

"Wayland Hunter, you have the right to remain silent. Anything you say can and will be used against you in a court of law. You have the right to an attorney. If you can't afford an attorney, one will be appointed to you. Do you understand?"

As Wayland indicated yes to Gevan's question, Nick walked closer to the glass that overlooks the office floor and drew open the blinds. There were cops everywhere! He motioned for some assistance to come upstairs where we were. Nick walked over to me and touched my arm.

"It's all over now Raven. You did a wonderful job."

"O.K" I said, trembling.

Two police officers stormed inside the office. Nick instructed one to recover and bag Elizabeth's gun for evidence, and the other retrieved Elizabeth from the locked file cabinet. She was escorted out of the room. Gevan went inside of Wayland's desk drawer for what he suspected was a weapon waiting.

"I want to call my lawyer." Wayland demanded. "You two keystone cops are going to pay for this shit. I'll see to it."

"Are you threatening us?" Nick asked smiling.

"All I'm saying is that you guys are making a huge mistake!"

"Save it Wayland." Gevan said. "You are under arrest for mail, tax, and wire fraud, first degree murder of Richard Hartley, attempted murder, among other charges that you'll be told of at booking."

Wayland smiled, although the perspiration on his forehead told the true story of his anxiety.

"This sounds as though you've been listening to the fairy tales of this bitch." Wayland said, looking towards me.

"Watch your mouth." Nick said.

"It's bad enough that you barge into my office under false pretenses and accuse me of fraud, but murder of my own brother-in-law?" Wayland said, as though he were hurt by the thought. "How absurd. You have no proof of anything." he said in a smug voice with a cunning expression on his face.

"Really?" Nick said.

He reached into his jacket pocket and pulled out Jerome's recorder. He pushed play and Wayland's voice could be heard confessing. His face turned pale and his knees buckled. Nick turned off the recorder.

"Get this trash out of my face." Nick demanded.

Gevan walked Wayland across the room. Before exiting, he paused and looked back at me, his eyes cold and unforgiving. A chill went through me.

"C'mon," Nick yelled, "get his ass outta here!"

Gevan jerked him forward and they proceeded out of the door and out of KIF.

"We won't need you to come down right away Raven, so why don't I have one of my men drop you home. I don't think you're in any condition to drive."

"That would be nice Nick. Thanks."

Nick held my hand and we began to walk out of the room. Nick closed the door behind us and we continued walking toward the steep steps that would lead us to the ground floor of KIF.

"Oh," Nick said, "I almost forgot."

He hurried back into the office and immediately returned with the dvd in his hand.

"We won't be needing this."

He handed me the dvd. I felt so ashamed.

"How did you know about this?" I asked with my head held down.

"Wayland's not the only one with surveillance equipment." Nick said smiling.

"I'm so sorry that this happened, Nick."

I used what little strength I had left to break the dvd in two... destroying this phase of my life forever. .

Chapter 24:

The voices of restless prisoners yelling obscenities was all that Wayland could hear. Wayland escorted by a guard, walked down the long, dreary-grey halls, carrying his folded bed linen in his outstretched arms. Through legal maneuvering, Wayland managed to postpone this day for about three months. Today, however, was the day of reckoning.

Retribution to KIF's clients will be a long time coming, if at all. The federal government had made it clear during the trial that they will be paid all back taxes FIRST before anyone else receives any money. It seems as though every "institution" is more important than the individual, specifically those clients of KIF. If those "institutions" don't receive the money owed to them, they still live to see another day. Not the case with most of KIF's clients whose life savings are involved. So the list of creditors BEFORE the KIF clients receive their money continues to grow: the federal government, all state governments in the various locations where he had operations set up, including Atlanta, business corporations, then lastly the KIF clients. How sad.

Wayland and the guard arrived at the last cell at the end of the hall. There was a glimmer of light that filtered into the cell from a nearby window. This is to be Wayland's home for the next few years. The guard opened the cell door. Wayland could see that a big, black man was already occupying the top bunk.

"Carma", the guard yelled out, "you got a roommate. Get up."

"Fuck you!" Carma replied.

The guard laughed. Wayland sheepishly walked in, not wanting to be left alone here with this angry young man.

"The bottom bunk is yours Hunter." the guard said, and slammed shut the bars to the cell behind Wayland.

The guard walked away slamming other bar doors as he passed, securing the corridor. As he dressed his bed, Wayland wasn't sure what to say, so he said nothing. He laid back on his pillow, and watched the impression of the huge man laying in the bunk overhead. Wayland let out a big sigh and wondered to himself was it all worth this? Was all the scheming and scamming for all these years worth being locked away like a caged animal? He slowly closed his eyes and smiled. He thought of the millions of dollars he'd hidden in wait for his release from prison. His smile grew wider. It didn't matter to Wayland that his sentence was for four years, or six years, or even 10 years. He figured that he'd be on his good behavior and probably receive an early release date. A small price to pay for the pot of gold; the well hidden pot of gold. Wayland became so distracted by his thoughts of money and "winning the game", that he didn't hear Carma talking to him.

"Are you deaf man or what?" Carma said in a booming voice.

"What? Huh?" Wayland asked. "I didn't hear your question."

"I said I heard the guard call you Hunter."

"That's right." Wayland replied.

"Is that a first name, last name, or occupation?" Carma asked. Wayland smiled.

"Last. My first name is Wayland. Wayland Hunter."

"What did you say?" Carma asked, as he slowly sat up in bed.

Wayland was afraid to repeat his name, but even more fearful not to.

"I said Wayland… Wayland Hunter."

Carma jumped down onto the floor to look at Wayland. Wayland, who had been lying down, immediately sat up to face Carma, who was now laughing aloud.

"My Dad used to tell me that GOD was good; now I see that he was absolutely right." Carma said with an unusual smile on his face.

"What's going on man?" Wayland asked nervously.

"What's gong on?" Carma repeated. "Let's just call it your retrial, with me being judge and motherfuckin' jury."

"Man, I don't have no beef with you! I don't even know you!" Wayland said, afraid.

"Yeah, but I know you, man."

By this time, Wayland's brow was furrowed, not sure what delusions Carma was experiencing.

"Have they put me in with a mental patient?" Wayland thought.

"Ronald is my given name, Wayland Hunter. Ronald Higgenbotham. Ring any bells?"

Wayland, now recognizing the last name, had the look of terror on his face.

"You know", Carma said, "that's probably the look my old man had on his face when he realized that you fucked him out of his life savings."

"Wait a minute Carma", Wayland stammered. "I can explain…"

"Too late for all that shit now bitch".

Carma motioned nearer to Wayland.

"He was a good, decent man who worked hard ALL of his life! He didn't deserve that kind of treatment… from no one!"

"Guard! Guard!" Wayland shouted.

Carma struck Wayland across the jaw with his fist. He then placed his broad hand over Wayland's mouth to muffle his screams, while squeezing his neck with the other. Wayland was dazed by the punch, his lip split and bleeding, never having a chance to retaliate, not that he could with Carma. Wayland's cries now blended in like a chorus with all the other screams from the cells. Carma forced him back onto the mattress. Wayland tried to fight back, but Carma's strength was unmatched.

"From this day on, bitch, you'll be the hunted." Carma said in a menacing whisper. "Now, we'll see how much YOU like being fucked against your will."

Wayland struggled to escape Carma's grasp, but couldn't. Carma was too big and too powerful. Tears welled in Wayland's eyes as he tried pleading.

"Don't cry NOW motherfucker."

Carma flipped Wayland over, face down onto the mattress in one quick move. He whispered into Wayland's ear.

"My street name is Carma for a reason, homes. What goes around… you know the rest."

Wayland closed his eyes, unable to fend off his attacker, and finally understood his fate.